DOUBLE CROSS

DOUBLE
CROSS

•

Jack Lewis

AVALON BOOKS
NEW YORK

PRINTED IN THE UNITED STATES OF AMERICA
ON ACID-FREE PAPER
BY HADDON CRAFTSMEN, BLOOMSBURG, PENNSYLVANIA

This one is for Dana, a survivor in spite of all, just like her Old Man.

Chapter One

I had been on Samuel W. Nolte for what now was the second week, changing vehicles and locations from which I could shoot photos that would prove him a liar intent upon ripping off the insurance company.

I was working on an assignment basis for the agency that did investigations for NorthWest Casualty. The latter company carried the accident policy on Nolte. In spite of my efforts, I was certain Nolte had spotted me for what I was. Each afternoon, he came out of his house and used a garden hose to water the potted plants on his porch. At no time did he ever raise the hose above waist level, and he offered frequent grimaces meant to show pain. It was a good act.

There was a huge potted fern suspended from a porch rafter by heavy wires. This plant was well above his head. He made no attempt to water it during my stakeouts, but the fern was green and robust. On the sixth day, I had hidden my car four blocks away before daylight and set up shop in a thick hedge that edged the public park across the street from Nolte's abode.

Hunkered in there among the thorns, I settled into the job of waiting, as I had learned as a child while hunting on the Mescalero reservation. It wasn't at all comfortable, but one could indulge in what I supposed amounted to self-hypnosis to make the time pass.

It was mid-morning before Nolte came out of the house and began to putter about the porch, trimming his plants, fertilizing some of them. As he worked, he kept glancing covertly up and down the street. Finally, Nolte went into the house and came out, dragging a six-foot stepladder. He erected it under the hanging fern and went up the steps to unhook the container and carry it down to the floor. There he began to trim tendrils and loosen the soil.

I had shot up most of a roll of film and backed out of my hiding place, walking innocently across the park to my car. I left the roll of film in the appropriate basket at the detective agency with a note explaining what was on the roll. The rest of the weekend was mine.

On Monday, I was told, "The lawyers don't like it. You were too far away. Too many shadows on his face for positive ID. Get closer."

I didn't bother with the first part of the week, figuring Nolte probably watered and tended the overhead fern on Saturdays. Instead, I went up into the San Bernardino Mountains and went fishing. I didn't catch anything, but just sitting beside the lake, my back against a tree, dimmed the mad pace of the city down below. It was a little like my childhood on the reservation.

On Friday, I returned to Nolte's street in San Fernando and sauntered through the neighborhood. Camera in hand, I cast frequent glances at his house. Hardly an approved technique, but I wanted to appear obvious. The subject probably was watching.

Saturday, I slipped between some houses on the back side of his block before dawn, shinnied across a couple of fences and ended up at the porch corner of Nolte's house. I had made certain he didn't own a dog, so I was able to hunker down in a large patch of greenery. I even napped sporadically, one ear tuned for signs of action, but it was after nine o'clock when Sam Nolte came out on his porch and looked up and down the street, then walked out as far as the curb, craning his neck for any sign of unfamiliar vehicles.

Crouched in his flower bed at the corner of the house, I listened as he dragged the ladder across the porch and erected it. I gave him about thirty seconds—waiting, in fact, until I heard a grunt of exertion.

This time, I had a flash mounted on the camera. I rose and whirled around the corner to aim up at the figure on the ladder, forty pounds of pot and plant in his hands.

"Smile, Sam," I ordered. "You're on 'Candid Camera'!" He whirled and I snapped a string of negatives as he dropped the plant, then fell off the ladder. I didn't wait to see what happened next. I was gone.

I wandered into the detective agency on Monday morning, expecting smiles and congratulations. The two partners looked like morticians who had just learned the death rate was down.

"The insurance company just heard from the guy's lawyer," I was told. "He said someone trespassed to put a ladder on his porch, then tried to drop a potted plant on his head. They claim his injuries are worse!"

"You have the photos," I countered. "They prove otherwise."

One of the agency's principals shook his head. "You never know with disability lawyers."

I told them where to send my check. It was back to work as the only Mescalero Apache process server in the entire world!

You're going to ask how a reservation-raised Indian ends up in Los Angeles chasing people who are behind in their alimony or their car payments. There are also a lot of folks in the throes of divorce, but don't know it until I enter their lives with an order to appear.

In my late teens, I competed on the Indian rodeo circuit during summers between years at the reservation school. I had been good enough at riding broncs bareback and bulldogging steers that I was offered an intercollegiate rodeo scholarship at Sull-Ross College in Texas. My father, a lifelong cowboy who worked with the reservation cattle herd, urged me to take a chance, telling me what I already knew: "There's nothing here for a young man, except poverty and probably a short life span." That's a liberal translation, because he said it in Mescalero. He did that often, wanting me to remember who and what I was.

I did a couple of years at Sull-Ross, getting hurt a couple of times when horses fell on me and another time when I came off my horse to bulldog a steer only to find his horn sticking through my arm. It was about then someone explained that in Hollywood, a rider could get paid every time he fell on his head rather than for the hard-earned occasional win.

Danny Dark was a second unit director for one of the small studios, which meant he was in charge of filming the action sequences. He hired me for a Western in which I had to wear a long, black wig and dress in what they thought an Indian would wear on the warpath. I already had learned that directors don't like criticism, so I kept my mouth shut, fell off the horse on signal, drew my pay for the stunt, and went back to the room I had rented in a place that the tenants called Heartbreak Hotel.

The hotel was where a lot of blue-collar studio technicians, stuntmen, and Indian extras hung out, some booked into the hotel because legal writs forbade them to make contact with the wives who were in the course of shedding them. The structure, about as old as Hollywood itself, was situated not far from Gower Gulch—the corner of Hollywood and Gower—where all of the old-time movie cowboys used to congregate. The hotel had a bar and a coffee shop where the food had better taste than the 1930s decor.

It hadn't taken me long to learn the movie business

wasn't what it claimed to be. Producers suddenly were declaring Westerns were a drag at the box office, a great way to lose money. The current generation of moviegoers wanted multiple car crashes and people being blown up. Dynamite wasn't my bag by a long shot.

Prices in the coffee shop were reasonable and I ate there a lot. A number of the Indian extras hung out in the bar, but I steered clear of it. I'd had my problem with alcohol and I didn't want any more of it.

I was eating a bowl of what had started out as vegetable beef soup one afternoon. I was getting short of money, so I was looking for bulk and vitamins. The coffee shop was a bit old-fashioned in other ways too. Several racks were attached to the back of the counter, holding various condiments, as well as soda crackers and little plastic bowls of chopped onions, diced jalapeño peppers and pickle chips. The shorter the money, the more creative I had become. Even with the waitress frowning at me, I learned the right amount of catsup, mustard, soy sauce, and crackers to put in, adding onion and peppers for zest, and still keeping the mixture edible. The dill pickle slices I considered dessert.

A horse wrangler I'd worked with on my last film moved in beside me and we started talking about that job and how tough things had become. He glanced at my bowl still half full and asked, "What'cha eatin'?"

"Apache stew," I declared solemnly. He offered a nod of acceptance.

"Yeah, we've all learned how to make that," the

wrangler drawled knowingly. "Even Danny Dark's making the unemployment line these days. A'course, his service business has gotta help him keep his head above water'n times like these."

"Service business?" It's a fact of life that a lot of picture people have other business interests on the side to keep the bucks coming in during the bad times.

The grizzled old man tore off a hunk of bread with his false teeth and chewed diligently while I waited. "Yeah. He works with the courts, seeing that people get served with things like subpoenas, orders to appear and that other legal stuff. Some folks don't like adding grief, so he has trouble keeping help."

"Where's his office?" I wanted to know.

I phoned for an appointment with Dark, who said he remembered me. With proper directions, I found his office in an old building that had housed a supermarket before it had been cut up into office spaces. There was a central switchboard just inside the door and an aging blond who answered for all of the businesses in the building, directing calls to the proper cubicle.

"Who shall I tell Mister Dark is here to see him?" she asked, shifting a wad of gum from one cheek to the other. At least I think it was gum. It could have been tobacco or snuff.

"Charlie Cougar," I told her. "He's expecting me." She was looking me up and down, inspecting my cowboy-styled shirt, high-heeled boots, Levi's, and the buckle I had won in an all-Indian rodeo that seemed like a million years before. On most Western Indian reservations, men adopted the cowboy mode of dress from generations back.

"Cougar? Is that name for real?" she demanded, frowning as she inspected my face.

"Real enough." I wasn't about to explain that my mother had seen *The Ten Commandments* while she was carrying me. She had been impressed by Charlton Heston, who played Moses, and by the director, Cecil B. DeMille, who was able to part the Red Sea. That's how I came to be legally named Charlton DeMille Smith.

She dialed an extension and announced me. From there on, it was pretty simple. Danny Dark had a team of a half dozen process servers: unemployed actors, saloon bouncers, and a couple of women who looked as though they could get close enough to a man to slip him a summons.

I spent more than seven months with Dark, usually getting assigned to serve individuals who already had spotted his other agents. I guess he thought a full-blown Native American wouldn't be considered a legal-connected threat. He may have been right, because it seemed to work.

At the end of that time, though, I was burned out and maybe feeling guilty about being the bearer of lousy tidings. That was when I found out about the insurance investigating job and went for it. At least it paid by the hour rather than the job, as Dark had it laid out. No service, no money.

I didn't have my own ticket, of course, so I worked under the agency's state license. They offered to get me a concealed carry permit for a handgun, but I turned it down. Both as a process server and a part-time private eye, I was running into a lot of strange, even weird people, some of them bigger than I. However, if you're not aware of the legal problems of defending yourself under California law, ask any cop who has had to put down a felon in performance of his sworn duty. No matter who you are, pull a trigger on another human and you see a vivid, four-color reproduction of San Quentin in the muzzle flash. Sort of a preview of what's ahead.

When I walked into Danny Dark's office to ask for my job back, he already knew why. "Didn't like the detective business, huh?"

I shook my head, trying to appear cocky. "Maybe I just don't understand it. But I do know what your work's all about."

"Okay, I've got one for you. Incidentally, it looks like I may be on a Civil War film. Lotsa horses. I'll get you on it, if it works out."

"Thanks." I hadn't seen any mention in the *Hollywood Reporter*. We both knew he was lying. "How many of your people has the subject burned?"

"For you, it should be a cinch." Dark ignored my question. "It's an old lady out in Studio City. Seems she went to the hospital almost three years ago for major surgery. She ran up a bill of about fifty grand and never paid a cent. They want to get her into court and collect their money."

"Nearly three years ago? That means the statute of limitations is about to run out."

Dark nodded, frowning a bit. "Yeah. That gives us a little less than two weeks to serve her."

"What's this *us* stuff?"

It was an old gag about Tonto's answer when the Lone Ranger told him they were surrounded by Indians and would have to fight their way out.

"Okay, you have less than two weeks." Dark remembered the joke.

"Where's the paper? And I need a picture."

Chapter Two

The picture was hardly what I expected. It was not of a little old lady in tennis shoes. Nor was it a photograph as such. Instead, it was a picture clipped from a yellowing newspaper. The image was of a tall, sultry-looking woman dressed in as little as the laws of most states will allow for public exposure.

"What's her name?" I wanted to know, not bothering to look at the legal papers in my hand.

"Karen Cooley," Dark replied. "She used to be an exotic dancer, then she gave it up almost overnight. Soon after that, she got into one of the studios and learned the makeup business. She's got a lot of screen credits for creating monsters in cheap horror films."

"What studio?" I wanted to know.

"Doesn't matter. It's not even there anymore. Went

belly-up and was sold to the Japanese. She hadn't been there for several years before the sale."

"She probably doesn't look like that anymore, either." I unfolded the summons to check the address. It was in Studio City, just over Cahuenga Pass from Hollywood, but on a street I'd never heard of. "Let's hope she hasn't moved."

"She owns the property," Dark stated, then handed me a large manila envelope. "Here are a couple more guys you can run down, if you don't get to her on the first try. They should give you eating money."

"Thanks, Mom. Always looking out for me, aren't you." I made for the outer office, where Myrtle, the switchboard operator, was filing her nails.

"Welcome back," she offered, grinning. "We didn't expect you quite so soon."

I offered her an Apache grunt, hoping she'd ask what it meant, but she was smarter than that.

Before World War II, Studio City was thousands of acres of mostly tomato patches farmed by Japanese-American farmers and their families. When the farmers all went to internment camps as potential threats to U.S. security, a lot of the land went on the market and was bought up as investment property. When the war ended, the San Fernando Valley began to grow houses instead of produce. One of those who really made out was an actor named Russell Hayden, who had been the romantic sidekick in the early Hopalong Cassidy films. He later complained that he sold the land too soon and too cheap.

I used a city map to locate the street on which Karen

Cooley supposedly resided and finally found the house. It was a one-story ranch-style that had a small front lawn. The place was neat and well kept with what looked like a reasonably new roof. Unlike some of the other homes on the street, it didn't look like it was built more than fifty years ago.

I tried the doorbell and heard it jangle somewhere inside. I tried it several times, then tested the screen door. It was locked. I pounded on the edge of the screen, but there were no sounds of movement from inside. I stood there for a few moments, then decided to check the place out.

On each side of the yard were high, thick hibiscus hedges bearing bright red blossoms. Views of the yards on each side were effectively blocked—and vice versa. As I came around the rear corner of the house, I was surprised to find what appeared to be a large backyard. Much of the real estate was blocked by clotheslines that ran across most the yard's width. All sorts of clothing hung on the lines, but closest to me were a half dozen sheets on two strands of wrapped wire.

Suddenly, one of the sheets was pulled down to expose a white-haired woman who began to use both hands and her teeth to fold it. When she saw me, the corner of the sheet fell out of her mouth. "Who are you?" she demanded, surprised and maybe even a little fearful.

I gave her my best smile. "I'm Charlie Cougar. I'm looking for a lady named Karen Cooley."

"She doesn't live here," she announced brusquely, still wrestling with the sheet.

"Let me help you with that." I laid my manila envelope on the close-cropped lawn and stepped forward to grab a corner of the sheet, then followed her moves, folding it into a neat, compact rectangle.

"Why're you looking for Miss Cooley?" she wanted to know, reaching to the line and removing the pins from another sheet. I grabbed one end of it.

"A minor legal matter," I lied. "As an heir, she was left some money in a will, but we haven't been able to find her."

"How much money?" We continued to fold, stepping closer together. The white hair had a curious blue tint to it, and I wondered whether beauty parlors charged extra for the rinse. Then I noticed she was wearing white cotton gloves. As well as a faded skirt of some sort, she had on a high-necked, long-sleeved blouse. Below the skirt were heavy cotton support hose stuffed into battered bedroom slippers. But it was her eyes that caught my real attention. They were an impossible shade of blue that seemed to leap out of her face and challenge me. I recalled an old Apache belief that if you followed a rainbow to its source and dug in the wet earth, you would find a turquoise mine. That was the color of those eyes. Turquoise.

"How much money?" she asked again, her tone a little harder with insistence.

"I don't really know," I told her. "I'm just trying to find her so I can put her in touch with the lawyers." I glanced about. "I was told she lives here."

"Not so." The announcement came with a shake of the head. "I rent this place through a property manager. My check goes to him every month, so this Cooley woman may own it, but I've never seen her."

"Sounds like we have a batch of bad info," I admitted, as we moved on to another sheet.

"Well, there is one thing." She seemed reluctant with the admission. "The property manager told me the owner lives in Las Vegas. I didn't tell that to any of the other people who've been asking about her these past couple of months."

We folded the last sheet while I pondered all this. I had a chance to glance at the rest of the laundry strung on the lines. Something was bothering me, but I didn't have a chance to concentrate on it.

"What's goin' on Alice?" The voice was deep and stern and I turned to look at the man who had just come through an almost invisible gate in the hedge.

"Nothing, Joe. This gentleman was asking about someone named Karen Cooley. He says she's supposed to live here."

The newcomer was probably in his fifties, but had the look of one who made a serious effort to keep in shape. He had on shorts and a T-shirt that bulged with muscles, and his breadth made him look shorter than the six feet two or three that he stood.

"How long have you lived around here, sir? Maybe you know her." It doesn't cost anything to be nice, even respectful, to people his size.

"You're the third or fourth character that's been asking around the neighborhood," the man named Joe charged with a scowl. "There ain't no Karen Cooley around here. She moved out a couple of years ago. Now apologize to the lady and beat it!" He took a couple of steps toward me and I could see the scars on one cheek and his chin. He'd seen his share of trouble and I didn't want to share it with him. I turned back to the woman.

"Sorry to have bothered you, ma'am." I handed her one of Danny Dark's cards. "If you remember anything else, please give us a call."

"There's nothing for her to remember," Joe declared, eyes narrowed. "What are you doing in this neighborhood anyway?"

I picked my envelope off the grass, then grinned at him. "This neighborhood? I was just looking it over. We used to own it, you know."

Joe took another step as I turned and headed for the street. Behind me, the woman laughed, saying, "Leave him alone, Joe. You don't have to scare off every young man that comes along."

Back in my car, I wrote down the number of Joe's house, then drove to a 7-Eleven, where I found a pay phone that worked. I called Sam Light and told him I needed a favor. He asked what it was all about, and I told him I'd rather talk face to face. He asked where I was and I told him. He had an office near the *Los Angeles Times* building in downtown L.A., but suggested we meet at a place called the Smokehouse, which is right across the street from Warner Brothers studios.

I was walking across the already crowded parking

lot when I saw him standing in the shade at the door, waiting. I figured why he had chosen that spot rather than the bar. We had met at a meeting of Alcoholics Anonymous.

It was just after 11:00 P.M. by my watch, but the bar was filled with the loud and convivial crowd that owned the expensive vehicles in the parking lot. Only a few tables were occupied in the dining room and we allowed the maître d' to guide us to one against a wall. We both ordered coffee and settled down, eyeing each other.

Sam Light worked for a newspaper in San Francisco that had decided to set up a Los Angeles bureau and put him in charge. He explained that he obviously was in charge, because other than a secretary, he was the only employee.

"You said you needed something," he suggested, and I nodded, reaching for my manila envelope and extracting the clipping displaying the charms of one-time stripper Karen Cooley. He inspected the yellowing paper as he nodded. "I've heard of her. She used to be big-time on the burlesque circuit with the likes of Ann Corio, Tempest Storm, and Lili Saint Cyr. That was before you could see more on X-rated TV." We didn't have burlesque theaters on the reservation, so the names meant nothing to me, but I figured they had to be big in the business of bareness.

"I have to find her," I explained. "I have to serve her some papers, but the trail is cold. The woman who's renting her house says she may be in Las Vegas."

Light nodded. "They have strip clubs in Vegas," he acknowledged. I shook my head.

"I think that's all in the past. She was a studio makeup artist until Metropolis Pictures got eaten up. Then she just disappeared." Dark hadn't named the studio, but I'd known when he had mentioned it that Japanese interests had taken over.

"What can I do for you?" Light wanted to know. The coffee was put in front of us and we were given menus. He looked up at the waiter. "Give us a few minutes."

"Assuming that you news people do work together on occasion, I was wondering whether you could get into the *Times*'s morgue and see what you can find on her."

"They don't call it the morgue anymore. It's all part of political correctness, I guess. It has the same old clippings, but it's now the library." There was a note of amusement in his tone. He considered my needs for a moment, then nodded. "Is there any kind of a story here?" he wanted to know. "I've made some friends at the *Times*."

"I don't think so," I told him. "Seems she had some sort of surgery about three years ago and never paid the bill. The hospital wants to take her to court, but I have to find her first."

The waiter returned and we each ordered a steak sandwich before Light spoke. "I'll dig around. See what I can find. Meantime, how's your program going?"

He was asking about Alcoholics Anonymous. "No

problem," I told him. "I don't allow myself to get up-set, and if I do, I go find a meeting and tell somebody about it. I don't let troubles fester, and that's a change." There had been a period in my life when I would lie awake nights, contemplating ways to get even with someone I thought had done me dirt. Or maybe I thought that was what Apaches were sup-posed to do.

Sam nodded, offering a half smile. "The last time we talked, you were worried about asking for help from a Higher Power."

I shrugged, looking into my coffee. In the AA pro-gram there are twelve steps to recovery. That was one of them. "I'm still having some thoughts on that one. Some people talk about God, but we Apaches aren't much for labels. Those who go to church on the res-ervation are mostly Catholic. The rest of us consider nature as our Higher Power, but we don't put a name on it. It's hard to explain. I can't figure out how to ask Mother Nature to solve a problem."

"Do you ever ask her for peace of mind?" Light wanted to know, eyeing me thoughtfully.

"I guess I've asked Someone or Something in the dark of night," I told him. "When I thought I needed a drink at four o'clock in the morning, I've asked. I wouldn't call it praying."

Light shook his head, smiling at me. "Don't worry. It'll all come together. That's the reason we don't talk about God in AA, because everyone has a different idea of who or what God is. If we sat around at a meeting and debated that, everyone would throw their hands in the air in frustration and we'd all go get drunk."

Our food came and we concentrated on that for a few minutes before Sam Light said, "If there turns out to be a story in this, I want it first, Charlie."

"Agreed. Meantime, what's happening with your problem?"

"Carol?" That was the name of the girl he had left behind in San Francisco. He shook his head. "Nothing's changed. Down underneath, I guess she's a frightened person. Frightened of me maybe. Both of her parents were alcoholics. In fact, they died in an accident, drunk. She has a good job now, and the idea of following me through the jungles of journalism frightens her."

"You told me she was alone," I reminded him. "No family. You ought to marry her."

"What's that mean?" he was staring at me quizzically. "I don't want to be her mother and father."

"It would mean no mother-in-law."

"Cougar, you talk in strange circles."

"Not really. Among the Apaches, when you marry, you move in with your new wife's family, but you stay as far away from your mother-in-law as possible." I shook my head at him. "Apaches know that if you look at your wife's mother too often, you will go blind!"

Sam Light had a piece of steak halfway to his mouth, but he was frozen, staring at me over the tines of his fork. I shrugged and smiled at him.

"No mother-in-law," I reminded him. "Marry the girl!"

Chapter Three

As Sam Light drove out of the parking lot, I realized we could have met a lot closer to his office. My next stop was going to be the hall of records only a few blocks from Sam's building. Apparently, the guy known to me only as Joe lived next door, but he had seemed almost possessive about the property owned by Karen Cooley and the turquoise-eyed woman he had called Alice. That wasn't what was bothering me, though. His face, scars and all, looked familiar, but I couldn't take it any further.

The best way to find out who owns property is to check with the tax people. At least they know in whose name the property is listed and who pays the taxes. That office is computerized now and surprisingly efficient, but neither the computers nor the efficiency told me what I really wanted to know. The house next to Karen Cooley's was owned by something called the Cyclops Corporation—and the corporate address was Joe's home, which told me nothing.

I found a phone and called Danny Dark. He was not in, but I left a message with Myrtle, asking her to have Dark check with the office of the California Secretary of State as soon as possible. I wanted the names of the officers of the Cyclops Corporation. Dark was in a better position to handle that chore than I. He had a fax machine.

My watch insisted it was almost four o'clock on Wednesday afternoon. If I hurried, I would beat part of the quitting-hour traffic back to Hollywood. I glanced at the other orders to appear that Dark had issued me and chose one meant for a guy named Timothy Stann.

A note Dark had attached to the summons told me that the subject had moved out of his apartment and his current address was not known. However, he belonged to a team of iron workers that bowled every Wednesday night at a place called the Hollywood Pins.

Since Dark only paid for success, I was batting zero for the day. It was time to make some money. I drove out to the bowling alley, located on Santa Monica Boulevard between a supermarket and a one-stage rental studio.

I parked, took the summons for Stann out of the envelope and tucked it in my hip pocket, then made for the ball-and-pin emporium. It was still early, but I wanted to scout the layout before the bowling team arrived. Danny Dark had not been able to furnish me with a photo of the subject, so I was going to have to identify him one way or another.

Inside, I counted twenty lanes, but only four of them were busy. Like most such establishments, it had a bar with a half dozen stools and an adjoining snack area, where one could order from a posted list of fast-foods ranging from hot dogs to pizza.

I noted that the lanes had two customer entrances, one at each end of the building. I checked out the men's room to be certain there was no door there leading to the outside. That was about as much as I could do until the team arrived.

I ordered a cup of coffee and settled into one of the booths, where I could see who was coming in from each end of the building. My attention, though, was distracted by the cocktail waitresses. Actually, it was one of them, since there seemed to be a change of shift going on. The waitress, who looked like most Hollywood blonds, was checking out, while the newcomer was waiting to take over and listening to what she had to say.

The new girl, outfitted in the short-skirted, full-bosomed costume, had her long hair in braids, ends held in place by tubes decorated with what looked to be Sioux Indian beadwork. Below the skirt she wore pantyhose the same color as her visible skin, and on her feet were handmade moccasins with the same Sioux bead pattern. But it was her face that really drew my attention. From where I sat, she appeared to be wearing no makeup other than a subtle trace of lipstick. I judged her to be in her mid-twenties and realized she was probably the most beautiful Indian woman I had ever seen.

The blond headed for the ladies room, and the Indian woman turned to talk to the bartender for a moment, nodding and smiling at something he said. Then she picked up her tray and came toward me, apparently intent on checking with the bowlers at the other end of the place.

I was sitting there in my Indian cowboy outfit, which apparently caught her attention. She glanced at me and offered a half smile.

"I'll bet they call you Sweet Sioux," I said. That caused her to stop. She glanced at my coffee cup and I figured she was deciding I wasn't likely to buy booze, so why bother with me.

"Almost everybody I meet comes up with that same line," she offered, but she still was smiling.

"I could sing it. I know all the lyrics," I told her.

"I'd think another Indian could do better than that."

"Then what is your name?"

She nodded. "You came close. It's Sue."

"Good. I'm Charlie Cougar."

"You're no Sioux," she announced, her smile fading as she inspected my features.

"Mescalero Apache."

"You're a long way from your reservation."

I shrugged. "Aren't we all?"

She shook her head. "I'm third generation Angelino," she announced. "My grandparents came here from South Dakota for work during World War Two. They never went back."

"The Pine Ridge reservation." I offered a nod.

"You're ahead of me," she announced gravely, smile gone. "I've never seen it."

"Maybe you should. It's your heritage."

She shook her head. "I've heard all about the poverty and the prejudice."

It's still your heritage."

At that point, one of the bowlers called to her and she turned. "I have to go." I watched as she stalked away, my Indian princess.

My attention was drawn away from her retreating back by the sound of loud voices and laughter at the other end of the building. Coming through the door were a half dozen men, all of them big enough to make Godzilla jealous. Dressed in work boots, Levis and T-shirts, they all wore matching bowling shirts and had bowling shoes slung over their shoulders. Apparently, they had come directly from the job. As one of them turned, I saw the name of their union and local number embroidered across the back of his shirt. They were iron workers, and even at that distance I could see that each had a name stenciled over the left-hand pocket of the shirt.

I sipped my coffee as they checked in and changed their shoes. As they filed to the lane they had been assigned, I rose and slipped the summons out of my hip pocket, holding it against my thigh so it wasn't obvious. As they laughed and joked, choosing bowling balls from the rack, I sauntered close enough to make out the names on the shirts.

One of them, a big redheaded guy with a sunburned face, had TIM embroidered boldly above the pocket. That had to be Timothy Stann, but I checked the others to be certain no one else was named Tim. All of them were standing at the end of the lane, getting organized as I approached. But suddenly, they all were looking at me, scowling. Two of them moved in front of my man as though drilled. I looked past them at the big redhead.

"Mister Stanns?" I questioned.

"Another process server!" Red snarled. "Get him!"

I tried to reach him, but the other two closed ranks, cutting me off. I was supposed to touch him with the document in order to make it legal. I was still several feet away from him, when the summons was snatched from my hand and two of the iron men grabbed me, one by each shoulder, and lifted me off the ground. I had to have looked silly, my feet waving around, walking on nothing, as they trotted down the wide aisle behind the benches.

When we reached the double glass doors, the one who had grabbed the summons was holding one of them open. My two captors took me through the opening and tossed me on the sidewalk beyond. The erstwhile doorman stepped forward to drop the summons beside me. "Don't come back," he ordered. Laughing, the threesome went back inside, the doors closing behind them.

A couple of arriving bowlers had witnessed the

event, but neither offered to help me to my feet. They just strode past as though I wasn't there and stepped through the glass doors. One of them did look over his shoulder at me.

I reached over to pick up the summons, then got to my feet. I flexed various muscles and body parts to determine that the only thing damaged was my pride.

I was thinking too, about my earlier problem of seeking revenge. If I was to follow the AA teachings, I would walk away and wait for fate to take care of my attackers. But, first, I didn't feel that way. I wanted blood! Second, I needed to make this service so Dark would pay me. I needed the money.

It was growing dark by now and I went back to my car, where I sat for a while, thinking, then plotting. Finally, I got out and pulled a nylon jacket out of the trunk along with a battered Stetson hat that I used to wear on the rodeo circuit. One of the rules for the sport is that you have to have a cowboy-style hat on your head when you come out of the chute. I'd found it also was good in Southern California's infrequent rainstorms.

I put on the jacket, zipping it to hide the colors of my shirt, then I jammed the old hat down over my hair. Summons in hand, I stalked toward the building and entered.

There, close to the doors, a number of bowling balls waited in the rack next to the lanes. Tim, the minigiant, was at the bar ordering a beer, and hadn't noticed me. I rolled the summons into a tight paper tube and bent to insert it in the thumbhole drilled in one of the bowling balls. I picked up the ball with both hands, holding it close to my waist, the tube of paper hidden by my nylon-clad sleeve, moving purposefully toward Tim Stann. Sweet Sioux was coming from the other direction, several empty glasses on her tray. She glanced at me, then recognized me and halted, staring. Without pausing, I glanced at the bar, then back to her, shaking my head. She didn't move.

I was no more than five feet from my quarry, when I halted, lifting the bowling ball higher in both hands. "Tim!" I hissed at him. He turned and I launched the heavy ball directly at his stomach, yelling, "Catch!" He tried to ward off the hard black ball, but it caught him full in his well muscled stomach. The summons still protruded from the thumb hole and he had it in his grip.

"You're served, baby!" I snarled at him, then turned to run full-tilt toward the nearest door. I glanced back to see that Sweet Sioux was standing there with her mouth open. Then she began to giggle. The other bowlers were gathering around their assaulted fellow to see what was wrong as I disappeared into the night.

I pulled into a convenience store parking lot and called Danny Dark's office, leaving a message on the phone to the effect that Timothy Stann had been served and I would be in to pick up payment the next morning.

As I got back in my car and headed for the Heartbreak Hotel, I experienced a feeling of exhaustion. I tried to tell myself I should feel ashamed for reverting to the Apache tradition of an eye for an eye and any-thing else you can take. But I knew I wouldn't be lying awake that night, fretting over how to get even. Instead, I hoped I'd dream about Sweet Sioux.

Chapter Four

"You've opened a real bucket of worms, Charlie."

That was Sam Light's introductory—as well as accusative—statement, as I walked in. His assistant was off for the day, so he had to stay in the office. It was his turn to call for a face-to-face. He said it was important, so I had driven into downtown L.A., trying to ignore the decay of this old section of the city. Many shops and stores were empty, some carrying FOR RENT signs, while others seemed to be waiting for demolition and the next city renewal program.

Behind his desk, Light had photocopies of several dozen clippings piled in front of him. I looked down at the stack.

"This is all about Karen Cooley?"

"Let's call it Karen Cooley and associates," he sug-

30

gested, waving at the chair across from him. "Have you ever heard of Mac Calley?"

I pondered for a moment, then shook my head. "Name seems familiar, but I can't put anything with it."

"Mac Calley is—or was—one of the biggest racketeers in this part of the country."

"Is or was?" I slid onto the chair facing him, trying to make sense of what he was saying.

"He disappeared about five years ago. He went out to lunch one day and never came back. Sort of like what happened to Jimmy Hoffa." Sam pointed to the clippings.

"There was a lot of ink on his disappearance at first. Some people figured he had fled the country to avoid prosecution. Others were of the opinion he's buried out in the Mojave Desert or is maybe wrapped in a hundred pounds of anchor chain in the ocean."

It was my turn to frown. "I remember now. It was like that Willie Bioff thing that happened back in the thirties. Bioff had gotten control of some of the craft unions and was ripping off the studios, threatening to start labor trouble if they didn't pay off. In the end, someone blew the whistle and he went to jail. Some of the producers almost went with him."

"Calley may have been suckering more than one studio too," Light admitted, "but it was mostly Metropolitan Pictures. The word is that his demands, plus a couple of real box-office duds, broke the company. He disappeared before the grand jury could get to him, but rumor has it that Metropolis paid him more than a million over just one year."

"But what's this got to do with Karen Cooley?" I wanted to know. All I was trying to do was serve a summons.

"Cooley? Calley? Try it for size."

I saw where we were going. "They're related? Man and wife?"

Light shook his head. "Brother and sister. And Karen Cooley has been insisting ever since Mac's disappearance that he's alive and will show up sooner or later."

"Seems to me, if he ripped off that much money and was still around, he could afford to pay her hospital bill," I suggested. "She'd probably think so, too."

Light flicked his fingers over the collection of clippings. "You'd better take this stuff with you so you can study it. I don't know what good it's going to do you, but I suggest you be real, real careful. Calley has some totally tough people working for him. A few of them are still around."

He reached into his desk and brought out a large envelope, sliding the clippings into it while he continued to frown at me.

"There's one interesting thing about Mac Calley's disappearance. In the two or three months before he dropped out of sight, he had been turning all of his assets into cash. Among other things, he owned a couple of nightclubs and a talent agency. He owned a haberdashery here in Hollywood that didn't want to sell anything. Go in to buy a few pair of socks and they'd discourage the sale, knowing they'd have to go and buy more to make the display look right. At least, that's what I've been told by some of the *Times* reporters.

"What was it a cover for?" I asked.

"Gambling in the back room. And I hear it's still in operation. With or without Mac Calley."

"What about Karen? Could she be running it?"

He extended the envelope toward me and I took it. "Go read this stuff, then we'll talk. There's some kind of story in all this. I just haven't come up with the angle yet."

"If you figure out what it is, let me know," I suggested.

"Carol called while I was at the *Times* getting this stuff for you. I have to call her back. Go!"

Thus dismissed, I went back to the hotel and spread out the clippings on my bed, then pulled up the room's lone chair so I could put them in some sort of chronological order.

There was a feature datelined nearly ten years earlier about the Calleys, brother and sister. They had come out of a tough section of East Los Angeles that was mostly Mexican. It was made obvious that a couple of Irish kids would have to be both smart and tough to reach maturity in those environs. Without actually calling Calley a crook, the writer let it be known that he'd had numerous appearances in criminal court for crimes that ranged from fraud to hijacking. There was even vague mention of a couple of murders, but nothing had ever been proven. In fact, he hadn't even been charged.

Mac Calley apparently took his big brother role seriously, for he raised all sorts of hell when his sister announced she was going to work in one of the lower-class burlesque houses on Main Street, but she had won in the end. The writer had pondered whether she had changed her last name so as not to be associated with her outlaw brother, or to keep him from being associated with her. The two may have been raised Catholic, but whatever the reason, Mac Calley was of the opinion that nice Irish girls did not take off their clothes in public—particularly not in a sleazy skid row environment.

A later feature story by the same journalist was centered on Karen Cooley. The writer discussed her fame as a stripper, emphasizing the fact that it was strictly regional. She worked Los Angeles most of the time, with an occasional turn in San Diego. She had a fan following, if that's what it's called, some of them driving the one-hundred miles between the two cities to watch her perform.

One reason for her success, the writer felt, was that she changed her act almost constantly, with new music, and new breakaway costuming, and did it all with a sense of humor. He felt Karen could have been as big as Gypsy Rose Lee in her heyday had she been willing to go east to perform. Instead, she insisted on sticking close to home and to her brother.

Then, at the peak of her fame, local though it was, she walked away from the so-called exotic world and

went to work at Max Factor's beauty salon in Hollywood. She was there only a few months when she
moved on to the makeup department at Metropolitan
Pictures. At Factor's, she had been charged with making customers—male and female—look beautiful, but
at the film studio, she entered the field of the bizarre,
developing makeup for a number of the low-budget
horror films that were Metropolitan's bread and butter.
It appeared that she had little or no contact during this
period with brother Mac, although in this same time
frame, he apparently was knocking down studio heads
with strike threats.

Then someone blew the whistle and Mac Calley had
been indicted on half a dozen charges. He had been
arrested, had posted bail, and had immediately
dropped out of sight. No one thought much about it
until the day he failed to appear in court. A few days
later, it was learned that he had been quietly getting
rid of all of his business interests, settling only for cash
payments.

A lot of people figured he was in Brazil, one of the
few nations in the world that does not have an extra-
dition treaty with Uncle Sam. It later was revealed by
government investigators that wherever he had gone,
he had taken nearly two million dollars cash with him!

At this point I knew more about the Calleys than I
really wanted to. I pushed the papers across the bed,
except for one carrying a newspaper photo. It was a
picture of Mac Calley taken the day he had been released on bail. He was about to enter the backseat of
a limousine, ignoring the photographer. But the man

holding the door open for him and glaring at the camera was my buddy, Joe! Calley was identified in the caption, but Joe was not. In the photo, he did not look like a chauffeur. He looked like a hood. But I reasoned one probably can be both.

I realized suddenly that I was starving, so I folded the clipping carrying the photo of Joe and his boss, slipping it into my shirt pocket. Downstairs, I bummed an envelope and a slip of paper from the desk clerk and wrote a note to Sam Light, asking if he could show the clipping to the cops and get a full identification and possible pedigree on Joe.

I addressed the envelope to Sam's office and tossed it into the mail slot. The desk clerk turned away from the key slots and handed me an envelope. It had Danny Dark's return address, and when I tore it open, a pale blue check dropped out. There also was a note explaining that it was in payment for serving the bowler. Since his office was only three blocks away, he had asked his secretary to drop off the check for me.

I handed the check to the clerk and asked if he could cash it, explaining that I would pay the next two week's rent out of it. I just wanted the difference. He gave me the difference, amounting to eighty-some dollars.

When I entered the coffee shop I noted the same waitress whose displeasure I had earned with my Apache stew was on duty, but all of the condiments had been moved out of reach and no longer were lined up at the back of the counter.

I sat down on a stool and crooked a finger at her.

Mouth drawn in a hard line, she approached and halted in front of me.

"What's the biggest steak you have in the house?" I wanted to know.

"The one that's twenty dollars." Her tone told me she didn't think I had twenty bucks.

"I want it rare. What goes with it?"

"Baked potato and brussels sprouts. Dessert and a salad."

"Sounds fine. I'll have coffee while I'm waiting." I motioned to the steam table behind her where the condiments and incidentals were lined up. "And bring all that stuff over here where I can reach it."

"Do you have twenty dollars?" she wanted to know.

"I have twenty dollars and enough for a tip," I assured her, "but the tip is getting smaller by the second."

While I was sipping the coffee, I saw Bob the Burglar come through the door that led to the bar. He looked a bit the worse for wear. He lived in the hotel when he had the money. I didn't know where he slept when he didn't. He spotted me and came over to sit down.

"How's it going?" I asked him.

"Not bad. I'm gonna be working again. Got on over at Columbia Pictures." When sober, he was a studio electrician, and from all reports, a good one. But those same reports indicated he couldn't stand success. He'd get a good job, work his tail off to make good money. Then one day, he would step back, look at the life he had created for himself and kick the props out from under it. That phase usually started with a two-week binge that got him fired. Then he'd sober up and it would start all over again.

We had talked a few times, but I'd learned about him mostly from gossip among the regulars in the hotel. I did know that Bob had been a machine gunner during Desert Storm and invariably relived his past military glories—real or otherwise—whenever he was drunk. That miniwar must have been the high point in his life. The low point had been the time he had been caught burgling a home and had been awarded a year in the Los Angeles county jail. It would have been more, but a couple of people from one of the studios had gone to bat for him as character witnesses.

It was obvious he had just come off of one of his loser bouts. His hair was unwashed and about three weeks too long, he needed a shave, and his clothes looked as though he had slept in them.

"How're you fixed for loot right now?" I asked. He shook his head.

"Not well. Got about enough for a thin hamburger."

"Are you working tomorrow?"

"I don't really go on the payroll till Monday."

"Fine. I'll buy you dinner tonight. Tomorrow morning, cold sober, you meet me here at seven. I'll pay you fifty bucks for less than two hours' work."

"Who do I have to kill?" he wanted to know, offering a wry smile.

"I'll tell you that in the morning."

Chapter Five

Knowing I wasn't ready for sleep, I drove a dozen miles or so to a Walmart store that was open around the clock. There, I bought a small galvanized metal washtub and a hickory baseball bat. There were similar tubs in larger sizes, but this one was about the size my mother used to wash our clothes in by hand when I was young. We didn't have a washing machine. In fact, there hadn't even been electricity until I was in high school. She had chosen the small tub because it didn't hold as much water as the bigger ones. During our summers, water was in short supply on much of the reservation, and ours had to be hauled for as much as fourteen miles.

I put the tub in the trunk of my car and tossed the bat in the backseat. I glanced at my watch and saw it was not quite eleven o'clock. In that moment, I realized that my main reason for coming out had been to stop by the bowling alley and try to talk to Sweet Sioux.

When I walked in, only three lanes were busy and the lights were off over the others. The bar was deserted, except for Sue and the bartender. I eased onto a chair in the snack bar as the girl watched me speculatively. Then she said something to the bartender and walked toward me, serving tray in hand.

"You're back. How much trouble did you bring with you?" Her tone was severe, but she was unable to hide the amused sparkle in her eyes.

"No trouble. Just me. And I don't bring trouble. It just follows me."

She motioned to the snack stand, shaking her head. "The girl that runs this has a sick kid. She went home early. Maybe I can get you something."

"Just a cup of coffee and maybe some conversation."

"The bartender has a pot. Maybe he'll talk to you too."

"Sweet Sioux, get it through your head that I am madly, passionately in love with you. We should decide what we're going to do about it."

She laughed then. "Are all Apaches like you? Crazy?" She didn't wait for an answer. "I'll get your coffee."

I watched her as she walked away. She wore the same costume as before, but tonight the braid binders and moccasins were a bright red, with different bead patterns. Moments later, she returned with my coffee.

"You take it black. Right?"

"You noticed the other night," I marveled, motioning to the chair on the opposite side of the table. "You're not busy. Sit down."

"I can't. We're not allowed to consort with the customers."

"Consort? That's an odd word. Where do you go to college?"

"Cal State Northridge. Computer science." She eyed me thoughtfully, cocking her head. "What about you, when you're not causing trouble?"

I thought about it for a moment, wondering how much to tell her. What would impress her most? "Well, I do a lot of work as a movie stuntman. If somebody makes a picture with Indians, I sometimes get to chase the cavalry along with every other Indian in town. If it's the other way around, I get to die maybe two or three times in a day. I get paid every time I fall off the horse."

"You were not chasing the cavalry in here the other night," she insisted, shaking her head.

"I also work as a process server. That means running down people, some of whom don't want to be found, and serving them with legal papers they'd rather not have."

Well," she conceded, trying not to smile. "Your technique seems to work, but how often do you get beat up?"

I shook my head. "Not often. I can run pretty fast."

She nodded. "I noticed that the other night. Why are you here now, Charlie?"

"I told you a few minutes ago. I came to see you and tell you I love you."

Well, now you've told me, but I have to help the bartender clean up if I'm going to get out of here at a decent hour." She lifted her tray in salute.

"Are you going to tell me what nights you don't work?"

"I don't work the nights I study," she offered with a short laugh and turned away. "Good night, Charlie Cougar."

"Good night, Sweet Sioux." I was wondering whether she had a mother and what the beliefs in her tribe were about mothers-in-law as I shoved back the chair and stood up. It had been a silly, meaningless conversation, maybe even stupid, but I had enjoyed every word of it. I wondered how she felt about it.

I was eating scrambled eggs, wheat toast and bacon when Bob the Burglar showed up the next morning. He sat down beside me and ordered a cup of coffee. When it came, he was shaking so bad he had to hold the cup with both hands.

"How long've you been sober, Bob?" I asked over a forkful of egg.

"This is the second day. Had a bad night."

"Stay off the booze and tonight'll be better," I promised him. He cast me a hard glance. "The first two days are the toughest."

"You know?"

I nodded. "I've been there. Meantime, see if you

can get down about three soft scrambled eggs and some buttered toast. Nothing else. I'm buying."

He shook his head, frowning. "You don't have t'do that."

"You're right. I don't have to do it, but in about an hour, I want you as bright-eyed and bushy-tailed as you're going to get today. Call it an investment."

He got all the eggs down and most of the toast without having to make a run for the men's room. As we got into my car, he glanced at me. "I've seen you in the bar once or twice," he ventured, "but I've never seen you take a drink. Not even a beer."

I nodded confirmation.

"You one of those AA people?" he wanted to know. "How long since you've had a drink?"

"A couple of years."

"How'd you stop?" he wanted to know.

"I went to Alcoholics Anonymous."

"I know that, but how'd you quit?"

"They have a program that helps you understand the problem. If you follow the rules, it works out. Some people don't get it the first time. Some never get it, but most do."

I kept my eyes on the Harbor Freeway, while he sat there, frowning and mulling over the information I'd given him.

"Why'd you quit?" he finally demanded.

"I got into some serious trouble because of being drunk. Then I just got sick and tired of being sick and tired, I guess."

"Yeah. I know how that goes." He cast me another glance. "You think I could make it? In AA, I mean."

I shook my head. "I don't know, Bob. It's not up to me, it's not even up to AA. It's up to you. You have to want to quit without reservations. You'll know when you're ready to call them."

Nothing was said for another ten miles or so as we both watched traffic. Finally, Bob gave me another glance. "Where are we goin' and what're we gonna be doin'?"

"We are going out to an apartment house in Carson, where we are going to serve a deadbeat with some very official legal papers. He probably is not going to like it. That's why I brought you along. I'm going to need a diversion and you're it. This guy is a very slippery character."

"Which one of us gets the baseball bat?" He obviously had seen the length of seasoned hickory lying on the backseat.

As we drove, I explained the morning's program to him. Our target for today was a rock musician who had walked away from a legally binding contract, and now he was being sued. Several earlier efforts had been made to serve him by members of Danny Dark's crew and nothing had worked. Now it was down to us. The fact that I made it sound like a team effort in my explanation caused Bob to look a little less ill.

We found Carson, which is in an area of oil refineries and has its very own smog belt, then we found the street on which the musician lived. Finally, we found the two-story apartment house. In the parking lot was a classic Buick convertible that was painted a bright hue of purple. From the profile Danny Dark had given me, I knew it belonged to our guitar plucker. I parked and surveyed the scene for a few moments.

"What now?" my aide wanted to know. I glanced at him and saw that he appeared a little less green, and his breathing was almost normal.

I pointed to an apartment on the second floor. "This character lives up there in two-fourteen. I am going to take the papers and sneak up there and crouch down beside the door. You'll have the bat and there's a washtub in the trunk." I handed him the keys then. "When you see that I'm in position, I want you to stand by the rear fender of that Caddy and start beating on the washtub. I want it loud. You can handle that."

"I can handle that," he agreed with a nod. There was almost the trace of a smile on his lips.

"Give me a few minutes to get into position. You'll be able to see me from here. I'll wave when I'm ready for you to start the noise. Got it?"

Bob the Burglar offered his first positive nod. "Got it."

Summons in hand, I climbed out of the car and made a wide circuit around the edge of the parking lot to avoid appearing to be headed directly for the subject's apartment. Actually, since he and his group worked nights in some club in North Long Beach, I figured he'd still be asleep.

I climbed the stairs and crept along the balcony, wondering how many residents were awake and watching me. How many had already called the police to report a prowler or maybe even a psycho? It looked like that kind of neighborhood. When I reached the door, I waved to Bob, who returned my signal. An instant later, a reverberating sound echoed across the parking lot. It was a steady, monotonous beat like that of a war drum.

Nothing happened for several minutes, then I heard the locks being turned on the door. An instant later, the door was flung open and a character with long hair on his head, no hair on his chest and a set of dumpy-looking boxer shorts stood there looking out. The tempo of the beating picked up a little.

The guy's eyes suddenly cleared and he cupped his hands, swearing. "What're you doing to my car?" he demanded. The question was interspersed with some of what had to be his finer vocabulary of four-letter words. At least one had to do with Bob the Burglar's maternal ancestry.

"I'm tryin' t'kill it," Bob the Burglar called back. The subject turned and slammed the door before I could rise and hand him the papers. The thumping with the baseball bat ceased for an instant, but I waved a hand in the direction of the Cadillac and the echoing vibrations began once more.

An instant later, the door was thrown open again and the musician appeared with a double-barreled shotgun in hand. As he rushed through the door, I extended one leg in front of him and sent him tumbling against the balcony rail before falling on his face.

I stepped forward to grab up the shotgun, then

tucked the papers in the waist of his sagging shorts. "You're served, buster! Have a nice day!"

When I reached the parking lot, I unloaded the shotgun and tossed it on the hood of the purple Caddy. Bob was already in my car, the baseball bat clutched between his legs.

As I started out of the parking lot, I looked back to see our wayward musician coming down the stairs, limping, headed for his car and his gun. I glanced at Bob, who was wearing a smile of self-satisfaction obviously born of a job well done.

"I think I could learn to like this racket," he mused.

"You did well. Pounding on that washtub, it sounded like an Apache war drum the way it echoed through that complex."

There was a moment of silence before I noticed that his smile had become a full-fledged frown. Finally, he glanced at me, still frowning. "I wasn't poundin' the washtub. I was vomitin' into it!"

I offered him a long look and almost hit a school bus. "You were pounding on something." There are some things you just don't want to know about.

"Yeah," Bob the Burglar admitted quietly. "The fender."

"Oh, no!" I wailed, almost strangling on the words.

Chapter Six

I pulled up in front of the hotel to drop off Bob the Burglar, taking a fifty-dollar bill out of my shirt pocket where I had stashed it. I do that a lot so people won't have a chance to see how much—or how little—money is in my wallet. I handed him the bill and he took it, scowling at it for a moment.

"That's what I quoted you," I told him. "Fifty bucks."

Bob nodded, still staring at the bill. "That's right, but don't you have anything smaller? Like a ten?" He looked up at me. "I don't trust myself with that much money. It'd buy too much booze. Right now, gimme ten for eatin' and walkin'-around money. I'll catch you later on the rest."

I nodded and had to go into my wallet in spite of policy. I found a ten and reclaimed the fifty. "Get some more food," I advised him. "Something soft and bland. And go get some vitamin B-12 pills. That's how I always did it."

He muttered his thanks and headed for the door to the coffee shop. From there, of course, it was only a dozen steps to the connecting door to the bar, but I pulled away from the curb, not looking back to spy on his decision. It was his life.

At Dark's office, I left word with Myrtle that his wayward guitar player had been served, suggesting I could use the check. I also had her note on the message form that my expenses had been fifty dollars. I knew I didn't have a very good chance of collecting it, but it didn't cost anything to try.

Back in the parking lot behind the Heartbreak Hotel, I rescued the polluted washtub from the trunk, throwing both it and the baseball bat into the coffee shop Dumpster. I was tempted to check the bar to see whether Bob the Burglar had made his way past it or was seeing how far his ten dollars would stretch. But I didn't.

After practically no sleep and the stress of the morning's activities, I convinced myself that I needed a nap. In my room, though, the red light was flashing on the telephone. The desk clerk told me I was supposed to call Sidney Perkins. He was a director I had worked for on a television series about a modern-day Apache tribal policeman. I had doubled for the lead in most of the hard riding shots and the falls.

I called Perkins and his secretary rounded him up for me. It only took him a few minutes to explain what was up. The television series, of course, had been finished many months ago, and the lead had gone on to other things. But Perkins and the producer had figured out how they could get a few additional shots that would give them something to cut to. By editing in the new footage and tying together two or three of the half-hour shows, they would have a feature they could release in Europe and maybe Japan. I was somewhat surprised to learn that cowboys and Indians are big in those geographic areas.

Since the lead wasn't available, and I looked enough like him to get by in anything but close shots, they wanted to hire me for three days of shooting.

"I don't know," I told Perkins. "Getting to New Mexico and back adds another couple of days. Right now, I can't give it that much time." I was thinking of Karen Cooley and the fact that I didn't have the slightest idea as to how I was going to find her.

"We're not going back to New Mexico," Perkins said. "We're going to shoot it locally. You know, like Sam Goldwyn or someone said, 'A tree is a tree and a rock is a rock. Shoot it in Griffith Park.' We've already scouted the locations out near Mormon Rocks. That's no more than fifty miles from where you are."

"How many stunts are you writing into this thing?" I wanted to know. "I'm not getting any younger, you know."

"Maybe three or four saddle falls and you have to fall the horse once."

"The horse? The same one used in the regular series?"

"Yep. That's him. We couldn't find one to come close to matching his paint job. You'll have to use old Ironmouth."

That was not the horse's name, but every stuntman in the business called him that. He was a beautiful registered American paint horse with overo markings that had a tough mouth and didn't answer too well to signals on the reins. Or maybe it had just been lousy training. It used to be they could use a running double to pull a horse down or dig a trench that would trip him. Today, though, that's all changed. The horse has to be trained to fall. The one thing old Ironmouth had been taught to do well was to fall on his rider's signal. When you slapped him on the neck, you had to be ready to get off!

"Tell me about money," I suggested.

"We'll pay you a grand a day for three days," Perkins stated. That was more than they had been paying the original star. "But you don't get any residuals, if it goes to television as a feature or to videotape."

"I'm your man. What about costume? And where and when do you want me?"

"We still have the double costume you wore," Perkins said. "And you know how to find Mormon Rocks." It was a picturesque area right off of Interstate fifteen not far from Edwards Air Force Base. But they'd be shooting all of the action stuff silent, so the jet aircraft sounds or rumble of freeway traffic would be no problem. The sound of hoofbeats and other stuff could be dubbed in or just covered later with public domain music.

"I'll pick you up at five tomorrow morning," the director told me. "Be ready."

"I'll be here," I promised before I hung up. In spite of the money they were willing to pay me, this had to be a shoestring effort. By picking me up and hauling me out to the location, they wouldn't have to pay me mileage for my own vehicle. What I assumed would be a freelance, nonunion cameraman and his assistant probably would haul the equipment in their own van and a wrangler would bring the horse. I was a bit surprised, in fact, that Perkins hadn't suggested I rent a trailer and handle the horse transportation. I had in the past, since it paid extra.

I had to call Dark's office and let him know I'd be off the scope for those three days. He wasn't going to like it at all. In fact, I wasn't sure I liked it, either. There was something about the search for Karen Cooley that I found intriguing. Or maybe I was mistaking that for what really was frustration.

It was the last day of the shoot and I was astride old Ironmouth at the top of a long slope that was nothing but loose shale all the way to the bottom. This was to be the last shot and had been saved in order to get the standard horse fall and my saddle falls and the running inserts out of way and into the can, as the saying goes. I had demanded they schedule it that way, because I didn't like the looks of that shale slide, and I liked it even less from where I was sitting on a barely controllable paint horse. If I got hurt, I wanted pay for all three days.

In the television film we were trying to match, the original star had galloped to the top of a gully, and paused, then ridden down it and into a creek bed. That descent had been steep, but was no more than twenty feet. There hadn't been much room for the star to get in serious trouble.

His ride into the gulley would be scrapped and my trip down the shale cut in. They already had shot footage of the slope from the top, showing how steep it was. That would be cut into the part where the hero paused at the top to look down, showing he was aware of the danger. What Perkins wanted was supposed to add to the spectacular action or some such. The slide they had chosen was at an angle of at least sixty degrees and was almost three-hundred feet long. Sitting there on the horse, I wondered if three thousand bucks was enough for maybe breaking my neck.

The cameraman and his assistant had checked out the route I'd be coming down. They had set up the camera and now made final lens adjustments. I was wishing they'd hurry. I was feeling less enthusiastic about this ride with each passing moment. I think the horse felt the same way. Finally, the cameraman nodded to Perkins, who raised an electronic hailer and pointed it at me.

"You ready?" he called, his words magnified many decibels. I raised my hand in signal. "Action!"

At the word, I jammed my spurs into the horse's flanks. More surprised than hurt, the animal launched himself over the edge of the embankment. When he hit terra not-so-firma, he realized the shale was moving

under him and began to fight it. He wanted to go back
up to where he knew it was safe. I was pulling on the
reins to keep his head pointed downward.

We had gone maybe fifty or sixty feet, when I knew
I was in big trouble. The horse was fighting the bit,
head high, and was almost sideways on the moving
rubble. I knew he was going to fall, and if he did, my
leg would be between twelve hundred pounds of fran-
tic, squirming horsemeat and countless tons of rough,
moving rock. That was a choice I didn't need.

I bailed off on the downhill side only an instant
before the horse's feet slipped out from under him.
With him just above me, I began to roll down the
loose, sliding rock as fast as I could make it. And with
every third or fourth turn, I'd try to see what Ironmouth was doing. Each time I looked, he was rolling
too, and with each turn, he seemed to be gaining on
me.

Finally, I hit bottom, where grass was growing, and
I staggered to my feet in an effort to get out of the
way of the rolling horse. As the animal hit bottom, he
began to struggle to his feet.

"Keep going," Perkins screamed. "Get on him and
ride!"

It was an effort to keep from looking at the director
and thus spoiling the shot, but I managed. Instead, I
hobbled over to the horse, gathered up the loose reins
and somehow levered myself into the saddle. I tight-
ened my legs on the horse's trunk and he managed to
get into a stiff-legged, shambling lope. With each of
his steps, I could feel the raw edges of his ribs grind-

ing against each other. I figured we looked like the
lone survivors of a wild horse stampede, as we rode
into what was that day's setting sun.

"Cut!" the director finally shouted. I pulled up Ironmouth, dismounted and led him back to where the
horse wrangler was waiting. I handed him the reins,
suppressing a grimace of pain. The wrangler paid no
attention to me. He owned the horse and began to look
him over to determine how badly he might have been
injured. Horses are more easily damaged than most
folks know. Think about it: all that weight on four
skinny legs.

"Are you hurt?" Sid Perkins wanted to know. I
turned to glance at him. Behind him, the cameraman
and assistant were removing the magazine from the
camera.

"A couple of broken ribs, again, I think." I was
clutching my left side. From experience, I knew my
diagnosis was right. Three of them had been broken
before.

"That was spectacular, Charlie," Sidney Perkins enthused. "Truly spectacular." He stepped closer and I
thought he was going to clap me on the back.

"Fine," I agreed through pain-clenched teeth. "How
about some spectacular money?"

Perkins shook his head, taking a step to the rear.
"Come on, Charlie. You know our deal."

"That was before I knew about the shale slide."

"Besides, the last part wasn't that spectacular," he
countered. "You and the horse both looked like you
were on the way to the glue factory."

"Okay," I told him. "You'll get my doctor's bill."

I'd had enough of Sidney Perkins and his shoestring production for that day. I told him I'd ride back to town with the wrangler and the horse, reminding him that he knew where to send the check. He acted insulted when I added that I didn't want to have to come after the money.

In the truck with the wrangler, I was thankful he was the strong, silent type. I tried to stabilize my ribs against the potholes in the dirt road until we reached the freeway, but I also was trying to recall exactly what was going through my head as I had been rolling down the shale slide. Something important. Something I remembered.

Then it came to me. As I rolled, there had been the flashing of white sheets passing before my eyes, then clothes pinned to a line behind the sheets. It was the thing I had noted the day I found the old lady under the clothesline. She was wearing those ugly support hose, a high-necked shirt of some kind, and thin white gloves. But the rest of the stuff hanging on the line was not the clothing of an old lady. There was no support hose and the undies looked like something a young woman might wear on her honeymoon.

Alice, or whatever the old lady's name was, had been doing the laundry of a much younger woman. She had known all along where to find the missing Karen Cooley! I was certain of that. Maybe she knew where to find Mac Calley, as well.

Chapter Seven

The wrangler introduced himself as Red Peters as I helped him load old Ironmouth in the horse trailer, then threw my gear bag in the bed of the pickup truck. I remembered Peters and his horse from the original television series, of course, but I hadn't been able to recall his name during our three days of filming.

Red was worried about the big paint horse. We pulled off the freeway a couple of times, and he went into the trailer to check on how the animal was doing.

The last time, he came back into the cab shaking his head. "Seems to be okay, but he's prob'ly gonna be mighty stove up for a few days. I was scared for both of you when you came tumblin' down that rock slide."

"No more scared than me and the horse," I offered, trying not to groan.

"Did I hear you say you're livin' at the Heartbreak Hotel? I'll drop you there." Everybody seemed to know the place. Maybe he'd stayed there from time to time.

"No," I told him. "There's a twenty-four-hour emergency clinic about a block from the Hollywood police station. Just drop me at the Cahuenga off-ramp. I can make it down from there."

"No chance," he shook his head. "I'll drop you at th' door. You don't need to be waltzin' around town with them ribs. They can be dangerous."

I knew what he meant. Sometimes a broken rib will get shoved far enough inward that it punctures a lung. I'd never had that happen, but I saw it in a rodeo arena once, when a bull rider had been stepped on by a twelve-hundred-pound bull. He hadn't lived to make it to the hospital.

"I'm not that bad," I told him. "All they'll do is tape me up and give me some painkillers."

"Doesn't hurt to be sure," he insisted.

True to his word, he pulled up in front of the clinic and extended his hand. "Sorry old Spots lamed you up, Charlie. He can be some stubborn." He shook his head. "Guess he's a lot handsomer than he is smart."

I stood on the curb for a moment after grabbing my bag, and watched him drive to the corner and turn back toward the freeway. He had a little spread out toward Riverside, he'd told me. Most wranglers blame the rider, not their horses, if something goes wrong. I wouldn't mind working with him some more, but not with that paint!

There was a big purple bruise across my back and right side. The young intern manning the place that night decided we'd better take some X-rays, so we did. A few minutes later, he came back with the film, scowling.

"Those ribs have taken a real beating, cowboy. Looks like you've broken them in almost the same place at least twice before."

I shrugged, which was a mistake. Even that minor tightening of muscles hurt. "Goes with the job," I told him. As expected, he wrapped an elastic bandage around my trunk from waist almost to my armpits, then gave me a brown plastic bottle with some white pills and a prescription.

"These will get you through the night," he promised, "but you ought to get this prescription filled tomorrow. What about the billing?"

"I'll take care of it now," I told him. "Just give me a receipt. I'll settle with the company."

It wasn't bad. Just a little over a hundred bucks, which I had on me. The intern called me a cab and I made it to my room in the hotel, too tired and beat up to worry about food.

I tried to sleep, but it wasn't working, and I finally took two of the pills, as instructed on the bottle. I was drifting away when I remembered that I had planned on trying to contact Danny Dark and Sam Light.

It was broad daylight when I must have tried to turn over in my sleep. The pain brought me up, sitting on the edge of the bed and gasping. I reached around with my right arm to grasp the area of the ribs, holding them tight as I started to cough. I was afraid I'd be coughing up blood, but that wasn't the case. I took two more of the pills I'd been given, then emptied my gear bag on the unmade bed. I pulled out a set of long cotton underwear that most stuntmen wear under their costumes as a protection against cuts and abrasions. I tossed them into my laundry basket in the closet, then inspected the heavy pads I had worn for the stunts. The knee pads and elbow protectors seemed to be okay and clean enough for another use. If I'd known that horse was going to fall on that slide, I'd have been wearing shoulder pads and a padded belt to protect my kidneys. Probably the most useless word in the English language is *if*.

I was hungry and had visions of a large steak and about four fried eggs. That feeling didn't change any as I unwrapped the elastic bandage and slid into the shower, adjusting the water temperature first.

Indians don't normally grow much of a beard, but I could feel the stubble and used the safety razor I kept in the shower to hack them down to skin level, using the bar of bath soap to soften them.

I managed to rewrap the bandage and get it anchored. The pills had dulled the pain enough that I didn't have much trouble getting into clean Levis and a shirt. I didn't want to bend over, though, to pull on boots, so I just rummaged around in my closet until I found a pair of reservation-made moccasins with rawhide soles.

It was almost nine o'clock when I finished the steak and eggs, wiping up the platter with a piece of toast.

I noticed that the condiments and stuff still had not been returned to the counter, but the waitress treated me with a bit less animosity than usual.

Back in my room, I called Dark Enterprises, only to be told by Myrtle that Dark was out of town and would be gone for at least three days. She added that she had been told to say the check was in the mail, if I called. "To offer a direct quote, he also wants to know where the hell you've been."

"It's a long, painful story," I told her. "I really need to get hold of him."

"I can plug you into his voice mail," she suggested. "He said he was going to check it several times a day."

"Okay, plug me in." A few seconds later, I was holding a one-sided conversation with his voice mail. I told Dark I had been on a picture, but was done with it. Then I launched into my recollection of the sexy looking lingerie on the line behind Karen Cooley's house.

"I think the old lady is doing Karen's laundry," I told the machine. "It would help if I knew whether Karen Cooley has a car, what kind, and what the license plate may be. Can you check that out from wherever you are and let Myrtle know? I can get the info from her."

Danny Dark had contacts in the local government and police department that I did not have. Had I set out to get the info I wanted, I'd be warned off with invasion of privacy charges at every juncture. That seems to be the way things go these days.

In books and TV shows, the hero always has some

computer nerd who can crack a code and reveal se-
crets, and it is only a matter of seconds before he can
give this main character a full rundown. In real life,
it's not like that. There may be real hackers out there
who are doing this sort of thing, but they don't have
much to do with anyone who even vaguely resembles
an investigator, cop or civilian.

I sat on the bed and tried to take deep breaths, figuring out how much exertion I could undertake without my ribs protesting too much. Finally, I gave up
that recreation and dialed Sam Light's office. The secretary I had yet to meet answered and told me Sam
was in Las Vegas for a long weekend.

"Is Carol meeting him there?" I asked. "Do you
know where he's staying?"

"I don't know." Her tone was ice-edged. "Mister
Light does not involve me in his personal life."

"Yes, ma'am. Thanks," I muttered and hung up.
Probably the kind of secretary everyone ought to have,
I had to admit.

Sitting in the hotel room was not going to produce
anything but boredom. The pattern of the wallpaper
was not going to change. I thought of checking on Bob
the Burglar. He might be staying in the hotel, but even
if he was, he might be working over at Columbia Pictures.

There was a noon meeting of Alcoholics Anonymous in the basement of a church no more than three
blocks away, but I wasn't sure I wanted to try sitting
on a hard folding chair for an hour or so. That could
be a danger sign, I mused, after making the decision.

Old-timers in the program always say that when you start thinking up reasons to stay away from meetings, you probably are looking for an excuse to get drunk.

I went to the meeting and it was only half over when I knew I should have stayed away. I had forgotten to get to a pharmacy for the prescription and the ends of my ribs seemed to rub against each other with each breath I took.

Finally, when it was over, I didn't hang around. I threw a couple of bucks into the collection basket and made for a drugstore that was located between the church and the hotel. The pharmacist filled my order, then looked at me when I asked for enough water to wash down a couple of the pills.

"What happens if I double the dose?" I asked him. He shook his head.

"The only thing I'm going to say is don't. You won't like it."

I can take a hint. What he had said was reinforced by the fact that the pills seemed to affect my depth perception. I nearly fell when I stepped off a curb a block from the hotel. There was no way I was going to try to drive.

It was mid-afternoon when I aroused myself from what could only be called a drugged sleep and made it down to the coffee shop. Bob the Burglar was there, eating a bowl of soup, the condiments lined up in front of him. Obviously, he had friends in high places.

"That the soup of the day?" I asked him, looking at the dark liquid with what felt like suspicion. "What's it called?"

Bob was moving another spoonful to his mouth, but paused to glance at me. "It's called soup of the day."

"But what's in it?"

He motioned toward the row of condiments. "Now? Or then?"

I shook my head and asked for a toasted cheese sandwich. "How's it going?" I asked him.

"Great. I'm still sober."

"Why aren't you working?" I wanted to know, suddenly suspicious. I bit into the toasted cheese to hide what might have been an expression of distrust.

"I am. We got a shoot tonight. I don't check in till nine o'clock. The cops are blocking off six blocks of Hollywood Boulevard for us, and we gotta be done before dawn. Paying us double-time for the night."

"How'd you like to go for a ride?" I asked. "I broke some ribs and I don't want to drive with the pills I'm taking."

He glanced at me. "Where we going?"

"Just out to the Valley. I want to look at a clothes-line."

He looked at me and shook his head. "You reformed drunks move in strange ways, Cougar. Am I gonna be like you?"

I laughed. "Not likely."

I paid for both of us, and he left the tip.

Evening traffic was building up, and I worried about whether Bob could handle it. He had a driver's license only because he didn't own a car. With some of the drunks he had tied on, he'd have lost the car, his license and probably his life several times over.

He slowed as we passed the house where I figured Joe lived and that I wanted to check out. It looked as though Joe was gone, as the windows were dark. I instructed Bob to park in the next block.

As I was getting out of the car, he glanced at me. "Want me to stay here?"

I shrugged, forgetting again that the movement would hurt. "Come along." He got out, locked the doors, and fell in beside me on the sidewalk.

We sauntered along the sidewalk until we were in front of the portion of the old lady's lawn that led to the rear of the house and the clotheslines. This house also was unlit, although darkness was closing in. Over the roof of a nearby home a nearly full moon was rising.

I started across the lawn, moving between the Cooley house and the high hedge that blocked the view of Joe's property. Bob was close behind when I came around the corner at the rear of the structure and halted. It was dark enough that it was difficult to see the lines, which were empty. I guess I really hadn't expected to find an array of sexy lingerie hanging there, but I knew that was what I had seen earlier.

Dominating the scene in the dying light were the two standard poles constructed out of what I took to be PVC pipe. The vertical uprights were of four-inch pipe, while the crossbar on which the clotheslines were strung was possibly two inches in diameter. Oddly, though, instead of the upright poles ending at the crossbars, an extension had been added to the top of each of them. Each appeared to be covered with a fitted PVC cap that would keep out the rain. The ends of the crossbars were similarly capped.

"My God!" Bob the Burglar muttered, and I turned in time to see him cross himself. "It looks like a graveyard!"

Looking back to the two clothesline standards, I realized he was right. Each of them resembled an eight-foot cross.

"I don't like this, Cougar," Bob whined on my flank, already turning back toward the street. "Let's get outa here!"

Chapter Eight

"What does Apache mean?" Sue Tallfeather wanted to know. She was leaning back against a tree, eyes closed. I looked up from where my fishing line entered the water of the lake to glance at her.

"It's supposed to be a corruption of the Zuni word for enemy," I told her. "In ancient times, we called ourselves the Dineh. That simply means The People. Actually, there are six—maybe even seven—different groups: the Western Apache, the Jicarilla, the Lipan, the Kiowa, the Chiricahua and the Mescaleros. Then there are those who say the Navajos once were part of the Apache nation, but after the Zuni beat them in a big battle, they decided to become farmers instead of warriors."

During my dissertation, Sue had opened her eyes

and turned to stare at me, half frowning in concentration.

It was her day off, and I finally had talked her into coming up to the lake with me. She had told me she liked to get as far away from the bowling alley and its bar as possible when she wasn't working.

She never had fished and wasn't particularly interested in learning, but she was dressed for the outdoors, California style. Her hair had been taken out of the braids and hung down her back, thick and sparkly almost to her waist. She wore a pair of faded denim jeans and a red T-shirt, as well as some of those walking shoes with all the padding that make your feet look twice as big as they are. But I wasn't spending much time looking at her feet. She was beautiful.

I had gotten a pole out of the car and thrown the line in the water probably as a matter of habit. As far as I was concerned, the real purpose of the solitude and the beauty was for us to learn more about each other.

"How do you know all this?" she wanted to know. "Is it handed down from the tribal elders? Is it written down somewhere?"

"Some of both. Then there are a lot of good reference books that have been written by researchers, non-Indians."

"Really?"

I shook my head, grinning at her. "Your Indian education has been sadly neglected, lady." I hesitated before I asked, "Is your family ashamed of being Indian?"

It was her turn to hesitate, then she offered a shrug. "I don't know. My grandparents—my father's parents—came out here for a better life and they found it. I think they were too busy working and building a life to spend much time worrying about whether Sitting Bull and Crazy Horse were right or wrong in destroying General Custer."

She shook her head. "They never went to any of the Indian gatherings they have around here. Neither did my own parents." She glanced at me, offering a grimace, then looked away.

"Too bad," I told her. "Everyone should know something about their heritage."

"Why do you say that?" she demanded, suddenly defensive.

"When a person's heritage is taken away, they also lose some of their self-respect. Pride in what they are."

Sue shook her head, scowling at me. "I think my father would knock you on your can if you told him he had no self-respect. If you feel all this so strongly, why don't you go back to the reservation?"

That question had come up before, usually with women who couldn't understand where I was coming from. I'd never seen any of them again.

"I can't," I told her. "I can't go back to the Mescalero. Not ever." I was staring at my fishing line without really seeing it.

"Why?" she demanded. "Why can't you go back?"

"I just can't." She had me on the defensive and the old troubles came flooding back. "Let's talk about you."

"No. Let's talk about you, Charlie. I know where my home is."

Eventually, I told her. I tried to gloss over the details, but that didn't work. It all came flooding out. I thought maybe my torrent of confession would engulf her, but it didn't.

After the rodeo season, I used to go back to the reservation and act as a game guide for the rich tourists who came to hunt our elk. That particular animal had been one Bureau of Indian Affairs experiment that worked in spite of early Mescalero opposition. Most Indians prefer venison to elk meat, with the result that the deer population never was allowed to increase to any extent. But the elk that had been trucked into the mountains and released flourished on the Mescalero reservation, because Indians were not hunting them.

A few big-game hunters heard of the mammoth racks some of the bulls carried and had come to hunt them. With the publicity derived from this beginning, the elk herd became a major commodity, with game fees as much as $7,000 for the privilege of a non-Indian taking a big bull. Everyone came to realize it was a good deal, because it brought money into the reservation, gave some of the younger men seasonal work as guides, skinners, and trackers. The hunting also helped to keep the herd manageable. Monetary tips awarded the Indian help by the hunters often helped to feed families through the harsh winter months.

I had done okay during one hunting season, then

lost most of the money in a poker game in Roswell. I was about broke, when I got the idea of trapping wild horses and selling them. It had been publicized that the reservation had too many horses and that they were eating forage that should go to wild game and, more important, to the reservation cattle herd.

I approached a member of the Mescalero Business Council and told him what I wanted to do. He thought it was a good idea and said he would take it up with the council.

This group replaced what once had been called the Council of Elders, but it had been done away with by the government late in the 1800s. The Business Council established decades later was made up of ten elderly and respected members chosen periodically by vote of the reservation Mescaleros. They oversaw the business of The People.

While I was waiting for the council to meet, a couple of my old rodeo buddies showed up, and we started drinking mescal someone on the reservation had made. When that ran out I rounded up some tulapai, which a lot of families made for their own consumption. This was made usually in five-gallon cans, which were used to soak corn in until it sprouted. The sprouts were crushed, then poured into water. In a week or so, it tasted like a weak beer, but the results were sheer disaster.

The next morning, I vaguely remembered that I had agreed with my two buddies that the Business Council no doubt would approve my request to round up wild horses, so there was no point in waiting. The three of us, still half-drunk, had saddled up, located the herd, and cut out about thirty horses. One of the riders knew where we could sell them in Roswell by the pound. They'd be slaughtered for dog food, the hides sold to a leather tannery.

One of the rodeo hands had a big stock truck he used for transporting bulls from one show to another. We loaded it up, then put more horses in our own trailers. We were just passing off the reservation when the tribal police came down on us, guns drawn.

We were held in the reservation jail, awaiting a meeting of the Business Council. I protested that one member had agreed I could round up the horses and sell them. In major problems that occur on Indian lands, agents of the Federal Bureau of Investigation show up to investigate the crime, but they were kept out of this situation. After all, it could prove embarrassing to the council member who had given me what amounted to his blessing.

When it was all over, the horses were turned loose to rejoin the herd, my co-conspirators were run off the reservation, and I was called before the council to be told that I no longer was considered a Mescalero. I had disgraced myself, my family, and my heritage. I should leave the reservation and never return.

My father would not speak to me when I went to gather up my gear and trailer my horse. I have not seen nor heard from him since. Another Apache had told me my mother had died.

"I'm not one of The People," I explained to Sue.

"But you know more about the Mescalero tribe than

most of them do, I'll bet," she declared. "No matter what they say, you're still a Mescalero. You were born there. It was a silly drunken stunt, and you don't drink now."

That only made me feel worse, because I knew what she said was not true, except for being sober. I shook my head.

"I may be an Apache, but I'm not a Mescalero. Except for the fact that one of the council was involved, they probably would have turned over the whole mess to the Justice Department, and I'd have gone to prison for grand larceny."

"But it didn't happen that way. You're here, sitting at the edge of a California lake, hundreds and hundreds of miles from New Mexico. You're future is here, Charlie."

I looked at her and tried to grin. "That's the way I see it too, except during the times when at about four in the morning I wake up and realize my heritage is being destroyed a day at a time. Real Indians don't chase people through bowling alleys. They don't invade backyards to see what kind of underwear is on the clothesline. They don't do movie stunts so people can enjoy themselves in front of their TVs."

"No," Sue declared with a grimace. "Maybe they don't do those things. At least, you were smart enough to see you were headed down that wrong road and found Alcoholics Anonymous."

She reached over and took my hand in both of hers, looking down at the intertwining fingers. "I like you a lot, Charlie Cougar, but I don't like you when you're feeling sorry for yourself."

I had brought her out to the lake with the idea that this might be a good place to see how she reacted to being kissed. I was still wondering what it would be like, knowing the place was right but not the time. There'd been too much heavy stuff going down in the past few minutes. I was staring into her eyes when the bell rigged onto the handle of my fishing pole began to jingle. I turned away and reached for the pole, starting to reel in my fish. And through it all, I was pondering what Sue Tallfeather had said.

Or maybe the things I'd finally taken out of my mental closet made me feel a bit better about who I was and why I was here instead of on a New Mexico mountainside, pointing out a big bull elk to a rich hunter.

The fish was a small bass that I carefully took from the hook so as not to tear up his mouth. I then edged down to the water and moved the fish back and forth just beneath the surface to get his gill action going. When I released him, he wobbled away, then seemed to gain strength and disappeared into the depths.

"I think you just proved something to me, Charlie Cougar," the girl said, leaning back against the tree, again, closing her eyes. "You would never have sold those horses for dog meat. You have too much respect for nature and the way things are. You just proved that with the bass."

"He was too small to put in a frying pan," I told her. It was disquieting to have a woman tell you things about yourself that you always had worked hard to hide.

I rose and started to pick up the tackle as she glanced at me. "Are we going now?"

"It's getting on toward sundown," I told her. "It'll get chilly real soon. Besides, I'd like to stop in Studio City and see whether a woman is at home."

Sue rose, pushing away from the tree trunk to give me a wry smile. "Is that the way you treat all your dates? Take her fishing, then stop off to see another woman on the way home?"

I shook my head, grinning at her. "Strictly business, love. And she's a little old white-haired lady who has to wear support hose!"

At the same time, I was wondering whether the Rosebud Sioux would be interested in making me a tribal member, if Sue Tallfeather vouched for me. I also realized how smart she was. She had learned much more about Charlie Cougar than he had learned about her.

Chapter Nine

The trip down from the mountain lake was quiet, neither of us saying much. I had no idea what Sue was thinking, but I figured my confession about being a horse rustler, and trying to steal from my own people, wasn't setting too well.

It was dark when we reached Studio City and I found the street I wanted. I was driving slowly as we passed the house where Joe lived, but the one next door was lit up in two rooms, which I took to be a living room and a bedroom. I pulled to the curb and stopped.

"What are we doing here, Cougar?" Sue asked in an ice-edged tone of formality.

"I am trying to find a woman named Karen Cooley, who owns this house. The woman who rents it may have heard from her. Cooley skipped a fifty grand hospital bill, and they want to get her into court."

"Fine," the girl said, lips almost a straight line. "I'll wait."

"You want me to take you home first? I was going to buy you dinner."

She shook her head. "We're here. Do what you have to do, but I'm having dinner with my parents. At home."

With a sigh, I opened the door to the car and slid out, pushing it shut with as little sound as possible. I didn't think I was going to find Karen Cooley here, but I was always as quiet as possible when attempting to approach a subject.

The door to the garage was closed and there was no window to tell me whether a car was inside. I mounted the steps and rang the bell, waiting. Somewhere in the back of the house, I thought I heard music, but if there was any other sound, I didn't hear it. After a few minutes, I tried the door, but it was locked.

I closed the screen without allowing it to bang on its spring and stood on the top step, looking toward my car. For a moment, I thought it was empty, then I saw movement, telling me Sue was still there, waiting.

I skipped down the steps and moved around the side of the house, taking the same route as before. The moon was full and higher than the evening a few days ago when Bob the Burglar and I had invaded this backyard.

Nothing had changed except the shadows. The supports at each end of the yard for the clotheslines were stark and white in the moonlight, looking for all the world like religious crosses. I could understand now why Bob had crossed himself at the sight of them.

I walked over to one of the PVC standards and tried to shake it. It didn't move, apparently anchored in concrete. The crosslike structure was casting a long, distinct shadow across the grass and, with my heel against the plastic of the pipe, I paced off the length of the shadow. Three paces and maybe a short foot. Of course, that meant nothing. As the moon rose higher, the shadows would grow shorter. Once the moon was beyond its zenith, the shadows would grow longer, but in the opposite direction.

"What are you doing now?" a voice asked. For an instant, I thought it was the white-haired old lady, but I turned my head to see Sue Tallfeather standing a few feet away, watching.

"Testing an old Apache legend," I told her, turning to take her arm. "Let's get out of here."

"Ghosts or something?" she wanted to know. I shook my head and pointed at the hedge.

"A very mean-looking man lives there. I don't think he likes Indians." I didn't mention that I felt he didn't like anyone else, either.

I led her down the side of the house and across the sidewalk. She had not locked the car, so I held the door for her while she got in, then moved around to the driver's side. I was just pulling away from the curb when a big Dodge van turned in front of me and drove into Joe's driveway. I stepped on the accelerator.

"Think that's the man who doesn't like Indians?" she asked. There was a note of amusement in her tone and when I glanced at her, she was grinning. I shrugged.

"I don't know and I don't want to find out. It wouldn't do to have the lady I love see me torn limb from limb."

That brought a chuckle before she said, "So tell me about that foolishness under the clothesline. Why were you walking down the shadow of that pole?"

"You've heard of the Lost Dutchman Mine in Arizona?"

"I've heard of it. I even read something about it once."

"Theory is that it isn't a mine at all. Instead, its supposed to be a place were the members of a Spanish treasure train were trapped by Apaches. They all were killed and the Apaches took the gold and silver, moving it to another site." I glanced to see whether she was listening. She was, but looked as though she might burst into laughter at any moment.

"Anyhow, an old miner called the Dutchman found the treasure out there in the Superstition mountains where the Indians buried it. He was coming into town with gold and cashing it in, not telling anyone where he found it, nor did he register the claim. He just came and went."

"Didn't people try to follow him?" Sue wanted to know.

"Yes, and none of them ever came back. The Apaches probably killed some and no one knows what happened to the others. Probably the Dutchman. In time, he disappeared too, and people are still looking for his horde."

"What does that have to do with the clotheslines?" she wanted to know.

"Well, according to something the Dutchman said once when he was drunk, the Apaches had buried the treasure near a rock formation called Eye of the Needle. When one stood in a certain spot and watched, at a certain hour on a certain day of the month, the moon would shine through the hole in this needlelike rock, and the rays would shine on the spot where the Apaches buried the treasure."

"It sounds crazy," Sue admitted thoughtfully. She no longer was on the verge of laughter. She appeared thoughtful and pensive. "All of this came from the Indians."

"No," I told her, doing my best to maintain a straight face. "That story came from a movie made with Glenn Ford back in the fifties. Apaches don't believe a minute of it!"

There was an instant of silence, then I felt a fist pounding on my shoulder. "Cougar, don't do things like that to me!"

I laughed and drove on for a mile or so before I said, "I'll still buy dinner."

Sue shook her head. "I can't, Charlie. It's tradition that on my nights off I eat with my mother and father."

"I thought you didn't believe in tradition," I chided.

"There are traditions, then there are traditions," she stated firmly. "Why were you pacing off the shadow?"

I didn't know why and I shook my head. "I don't know. Just something to do, I guess."

"Who is this woman you're trying to serve?" she wanted to know. "Why is it so important to find her?"

"Like I said, she owes a lot of money. If I serve her with a summons, I make what is a lot of money to me. Her name is Karen Cooley and she's an ex-stripper. Her brother was a racketeer named Mac Calley, who disappeared off the face of the earth a few years back. What disappeared with him was about two million dollars."

"But it's not him you're after?"

"No." I shook my head. "Just his sister."

Sue lived on a nice, quiet street in Glendale. She had been playing with her dog in the front yard when I pulled up that afternoon, so I hadn't had much of a chance to look over the house.

Parked in front of it in the brightness of the full moon, it looked like something off a movie set. It was a small cottage set back from the street on a big lot with roses climbing trellises on both sides of the front door. There were what looked like fruit trees in the front yard, as well as flowers flanking each property line. The lights shining through the curtains were warm and welcoming. It was nice.

"I'd invite you in, but I think my folks are already eating," she told me, as she opened the car door. I reached across her and pulled it shut.

"You're interfering with my training," I told her as I opened my own door and got out to circle the hood. "My efforts to be a gentleman need all the practice they can get." I opened her door and offered a slight bow.

"Charlie, you're crazy!"

She looked up at me smiling, standing close, and I knew this was the time. I kissed her and felt the warmth of her breath on my cheek. It was nice, and intimate, and I didn't want her to break away. I held her tight, until she pushed against my chest with the heel of her hand.

"Later, Cougar," she said softly. Then she reached up to kiss me on the cheek. "Good night."

I stood there. Maybe I was what they call dumbfounded. I watched as she moved up the sidewalk to the door and disappeared inside without looking back.

I glanced at my wristwatch. It was a little after seven and I wondered why the lights were on and the radio playing if no one was at home in the Cooley rental. The house was only twenty minutes or so away. Another check would not hurt a bit and I had nothing else to do until I could get hold of Sam Light or Danny Dark.

It was fully dark and the moon almost directly overhead when I pulled up half a block from the Cooley house. From where I parked, I could see that the lights were still on in the house.

This time, I didn't hesitate. I stalked up to the door and rang the bell, waiting an instant. Nothing happened, so I twisted the knob and entered, looking about.

The furnishings didn't resemble anything a little old lady in her sixties might move from one rental unit to another. Most of the stuff was made of glass and stainless steel, twisted into modernistic but not necessarily comfortable shapes.

But that wasn't what impressed me. What did was the smell of death. I had experienced it before and it's an odor you don't forget. There was a light on in the rear of the house and I went in that direction, until I stumbled over something. I found a hallway light and switched it on. At my feet lay a small white dog, stiff with rigor mortis. He had been shot through the head with what appeared to be a small-caliber bullet.

I shoved the carcass aside with my foot and continued down the hallway, the odor becoming stronger. The door at the end of the hall was partially shut, although I could see the light seeping around the edges. I shoved the door open and my heart leaped into my throat.

She was tied to a chair, a blood-soaked gag in her mouth, and her turquoise-colored eyes staring straight at me. From the sight of her body, it was clear that she had been tortured. On the floor beside her was a hank of white hair.

There was blood in the hair on her head too, and for a moment I thought he had scalped her. I finally was able to identify the white hair as a wig. I knew then that I had spoken to the real Karen Cooley that first day in the backyard, when I had helped her fold sheets.

Near one of her feet, there was a white sheet that had been pulled down from the bed. I bent to look at it and saw that with one of her bloody toes, she apparently had marked two X-shaped crosses on the white satin. Double cross!

She appeared to have been dead for at least a day. There was nothing I could do except call 911. I wanted to get out of there. To turn and run. Instead, I tried not to breathe too deeply as I looked around for a telephone.

Chapter Ten

I had to get out of the house, but the cops had told me to wait until someone got there. I was waiting on the front steps, wishing I had a drink. It was the worst thing I could wish for, but at the time, it seemed the right answer to all the stuff that was happening.

I had made one discovery and wondered why I hadn't realized it earlier. The little old lady who Joe had called Alice during my first visit was Karen Cooley. The big hat shading her face, the high-necked blouse to hide the fact that her neck still was uncorded, and unwrinkled had been a part of her disguise. The white cotton gloves and the rough cotton support hose that probably were padded were part of the operation. An old lady would have veins and liver spots on the backs of her hands, and the hosiery made her legs unattractive. I had not had a chance to see her face clearly, but it was smooth and unlined. When I interviewed her in the backyard, she had worn steel-rimmed spectacles that probably were clear glass, and a little makeup learned at Metropolitan Studios had given her that aged look.

I should have recognized all this, plus the fact that her voice had not been scratchy as I might have expected. There had been a bit of huskiness, true, but that could be from too many cigarettes or cheap booze. I also was willing to bet that if she had monogrammed travel cases, they were initialed with KAC: Karen Alice Cooley.

Sitting there wondering where the nearest saloon was, I had mixed feelings about Karen Cooley. I didn't even know her, but when you've hunted someone long enough, you get the feeling that you do. The fact that she had fooled me completely bothered me. I had stood around like a fool, helping her fold those sheets, while her sexy lingerie had been hanging in front of me.

A police vehicle pulled in front of the house and two officers got out. Both of them wore the uniform of the Los Angeles Police Department, which told me that Studio City was a rent-a-cop town. The city council had discovered it could hire LAPD to do the policing cheaper than they could afford their own force.

Years ago, Bob Hope described Los Angeles as "thirteen suburbs in search of a city." That still was true to a great extent. Many areas like West Hollywood had been county territory for years and came under the jurisdiction of the L.A. County Sheriff's Department.

I stood up then, holding my hands out at my sides so they wouldn't mistake me for a killer who had hung around for a go at them. They halted in front of me, the younger one produced a notebook and pen, while his gray-haired, ruddy-faced partner stared at me hard-eyed for a moment. I returned his look.

"We got a call," he said. "What's happened here?"

"There's a dead woman in the back bedroom."

"How'd you come to find her?"

"I'm a process server," I told him. "Charlton DeMille Smith." That brought a look of doubt into his eyes, and he shook his head. His name tag identified him as Terrell. The kid with the pen wrote it down. "I have been trying to serve the lady for a couple of days."

"She shot?" the younger one wanted to know. His name tag read Tucker. Terrell and Tucker. Sounded like a comedy act. I wondered which one was the straight man. I shook my head.

"Her dog was. Small caliber. Whoever it was tied her up and went after her with a knife."

"Stay here," Terrell ordered, and his partner nodded. "I'll take a look." The younger officer still held his little notebook, but he stuck the pen in his shirt pocket and took a couple of steps to the rear, getting clear of me. His empty hand went down to hook the thumb in his belt just above the grip of his holstered automatic.

Terrell came out and down the steps, face grim.

"He's not lying. She's a real mess." He looked at me. "You carry a knife?"

"Sure. Doesn't everyone?" I tried to grin, but it didn't come off.

"Let me see it." At his order, I dug in my pocket and pulled out the small buck folder I always carry. All horse people carry knives for cutting the animal loose, if it gets hung up. The handle of my knife had been inlaid with turquoise and silver, one of the semi-custom jobs Buck markets. It had been a Christmas present from my father several years earlier.

I handed him the knife and he opened the blade, inspecting it carefully by the light of his flashlight. He folded the blade and started to stick the knife in his pocket. "I'll keep this for now," he stated, daring me to argue. I did.

"Not without a signed receipt, you don't," I told him. "That knife has great sentimental value."

He offered a grimace, still holding the knife, and turned to Tucker. "Call this in. Tell them what we've got. And bring me a receipt book and the yellow tape." Then he turned back to me. "Know who she is?"

"I think it's Karen Cooley. That's who I've been chasing."

His eyebrows went up. "Karen Cooley, as in stripper?"

"The same. And sister of the elusive Mac Calley." I heaved a sigh. "How long am I going to have to hang around here?"

He shook his head, then handed me back my knife.

"Long enough that you may want to take up wood carving to pass the time."

That was the first time I had felt maybe I should invest in a cell phone. They weren't going to let me use the phone in the house, which they would dust for fingerprints, and I needed to call Sam Light, who should have come back from San Francisco.

The younger cop returned with the receipt book and the yellow tape. His partner pocketed the book and handed him the end of the roll of tape, which was marked with the words CRIME SCENE—DO NOT ENTER. Between the two of them, they managed to string it across the front of the lot, tying each end off in the hedges that divided properties.

"That should impress the brass," Terrell offered with a twist of the lip that could have been a sneer.

The brass was not long in arriving, two cars pulling up and disgorging men in plainclothes. One was a photographer, young enough that he must have been moonlighting to support his college courses. The others were older and tougher looking.

Camera bag in hand, he and two others went directly into the house, while another jerked his head at Terrell, drawing him away from me. They turned their backs and conversed in tones low enough that I couldn't hear. Finally, they turned back to me.

"Your name's Smith?" asked the older one who had a badge held to the front of his coat by a stiff insert in the breast pocket.

I nodded. "I'm Smith."

I had to repeat everything I already had told the two uniformed officers. Then he wanted to know more.

"You say she was disguised as an old lady the first time you saw her? Why would that be?"

"She knew we were after her to get her into court. She'd already burned a couple of other process servers."

"And you didn't realize this was not an old woman?"

I shook my head. "She was good. And she covered up every part of her body that would say she wasn't old. Her hands, her neck, her legs. She had the white wig and pretty much hid her face under a big hat." I paused, thinking about what I'd said.

"Check her eyes too," I suggested. "I think she was wearing blue contact lenses to add to the deception."

The detective took my full name as well as the Charlie Cougar handle, since I was registered in the hotel under that one. He had been taking notes on most of our conversation, but added my room number at the Heartbreak Hotel.

"You sure you weren't miffed enough over her fooling you to get even?" he wanted to know.

"Come on!" I chided. "This is a business. It's a job. You win some, you lose some. Am I going to get upset enough to carve her up and not get my service fee? There're no personalities involved. Get real." I won't say that I actually felt that way, but I wanted to impress my interrogator. The fee didn't seem important anymore.

He gave me an odd look, then nodded. "I guess that

makes sense." He closed his notebook and turned to Tucker, who was standing by. Terrell must have gone inside with the others, although I hadn't seen him leave.

"We're turning Smith loose," he told the uniformed officer. That brought a nod and the detective turned back to me, handing me a business card. I stuck it in my shirt pocket without looking at it. "You're a witness," he said. "Don't leave town without checking with me. And we'll want you downtown to make a statement. I'll call you on that."

The session had not been nearly as bad as I had expected, even though Tucker followed me down the block to my car and was careful to note the make, year, and license number in his little book. As I unlocked it and got in, he offered a wave and turned to walk back to the yellow tape barricade.

I sat there in the dark for a few moments, taking several deep breaths and exhaling through my mouth. I learned long ago such an exercise helped to settle my nerves, if they needed it. I had expected to be read my Miranda rights, handcuffed and hauled downtown to Parker Center for a full-scale interrogation. I was really surprised. Years back, the reservation police— my own people—had been a lot rougher over my suspected misappropriation of those horses. That had been my only encounter with the law—except for several arrests as a common drunk and maybe disorderly conduct.

I found an all-night Denny's restaurant, where I ordered a cup of coffee, drank part of it, then made for the phone in the back. Somehow it had gotten to be nearly eleven o'clock. I dialed Sam Light's home number. He answered and I identified myself.

"I know it's you," he grumped. "I'd know that whiskey rasp in a crowd!"

"If I woke you up, sorry. I didn't think you ace reporters ever slept."

"It's because people like you won't let us. What's up?" I could picture him sitting up on the edge of his bed and lighting a cigarette about then.

"Well, to start with," I told him, "Karen Cooley appears to be dead."

"What do you mean by appears to be?"

"Somebody's dead, but she hasn't been identified by anyone but me, and I'm sure no authority."

"Start at the beginning," he ordered tersely. "You're rambling."

"No. I'm just unwinding. I spent a long, interesting evening with the cops."

"Start at the beginning, Cougar." His voice was a little more kindly, so I gave it all to him from the beginning, although he was aware of most of it. I explained that I had checked her house out earlier in the evening, including the backyard where I'd first seen her. The lights had been on, but no one had appeared to be home. I'd taken Sue home, then come back, finding the lights still on. I'd tried the doorbell, then the door, finding it open. Thinking the lady might be in the back of the house, I'd started back before I caught the odor that goes with dying, then found the dead dog.

"I took a quick look," I told him. "Enough to see the white wig and the fact that the dead woman was not old. In fact, she was reasonably pretty until someone started torturing her. That was when I called the cops."

"Why didn't you call me first?" Light wanted to know. He was serious.

"Call it panic, if you want to. Or maybe I was just trying to do things according to the book to keep my tail out of a crack."

"In the newspaper business, there is no such book," he admonished. "Not much I can do tonight. If I sent out a photographer this late, he'd get a shot of the yellow tape and that's about all." A pause. "But I have one for you."

"What?" I wanted to know.

"The ugly guy in that picture with Mac Calley? That was his bodyguard, a guy called Joe Delaney. They'd been together since they were kids on the East Side. Started out stealing hubcaps as a team!"

"And he lives right next door to the late Karen Cooley."

"Yeah. Interesting, isn't it?"

Chapter Eleven

I didn't sleep much after talking to Sam Light, and the next morning, I phoned central casting from my room to see whether there was a call for genuine Apache Indians who could double as Mexicans, Polynesians, Eskimos or Orientals. If that possibility seems strange, keep in mind that a young man who used to do all the Polynesian pictures was named Ray Mala. He actually was an Eskimo. "Nothing now," was the standard central casting reply in my ear. "Call later."

I went down to the coffee shop, stepping outside long enough to thumb the required stray change into a padlocked metal stand and liberate a copy of *The Hollywood Reporter*. It's the daily trade journal of the movie and television business and runs weekly columns on films and television shows that are in the pre-production stages.

Over a cup of coffee, I leafed through the pages, but didn't find anything that offered promise. There was one film planned about a Mexican family, but they were going to shoot it in Mexico. They'd be hiring Mexican extras for a lot less than what we Hollywood types earned. I left the paper on the counter and went back to my room, where I dialed Sam Light's office. It was a few minutes before eight, and he answered the phone himself. His secretary didn't come in until 8:30, he had told me.

"Looks like the rest of the world didn't get the word on last night's events," Light offered. "There's nothing in the early editions."

"It was pretty late when I left there," I told him, "and no one from the newspapers or TV had showed up yet."

"There'll be plenty in the afternoon papers," he promised. "Got anything you didn't tell me last night?"

"Yeah." I had awakened during the night, thinking about it. "There is. Sometime before she died, she apparently used a bloody toe to mark two Xs on a satin bedsheet that was near her foot."

"Two Xs," the voice in my ear mused. "Probably stands for a double-cross. I wonder what that's all about."

"I have no idea," I told him. "I'm just telling you what I saw."

"What did the cops think about it?" Sam wanted to know.

"They weren't discussing theory with me. They were too busy asking me questions."

"Well, I'd better get out to the cop shop and try to find out what's happening. Every other reporter and cameraman in town is probably parked there now, and this thing could turn into a real circus. Karen Cooley's still news. In her day, she cut a pretty wide swath through this town, even if her brother tried to hold her down. Story is that he wanted someone in the family to be respectable."

"I gather Mac Calley cut his own swath, and look what it got them both," I pointed out.

"She always insisted he wasn't dead," Light told me. "She said he'd be coming back when things cooled off and the statute of limitations ran out on some of the charges against him. She even said once he'd turn up with the couple of million bucks he had when he disappeared." It sounded to me as though Sam Light had spent a lot of time during recent hours researching the Calley family.

"Too bad we can't ask her about all that now."

"Maybe she was telling us something with that double cross," Light suggested, then added, "think about it. I have to get out of here and do some work."

"Well, I'd better go see Danny Dark, if he's back in town," I told him. "I'm going to tell him he owes me. For all practical purposes, I served her. I left the papers right there on her dining room table." Actually, I didn't know what had happened to the summons.

Maybe the cops had it. I certainly didn't have it when I finally got back to my room.

Light laughed. "Good luck with that one. I hope Dark sees it your way."

Dark didn't. He had heard about Karen Cooley's death on his car radio and all but threw me out of his office when I suggested he pay me for serving the late lady—in spite of her noncompliant condition—with the order to appear in court.

"But I put in more time on this than on anything I've ever done for you," I complained.

"And you'd have been paid accordingly," Dark stated, "had you served someone who was able to appear in court. As it is, I get nothing. The hospital she bilked gets nothing. And you get nothing!"

"You're in a real great mood," I commented. "You must have had bad luck in Vegas."

He gave me a disgusted look. "I don't even want to talk about it. Go serve some papers."

In the outer office, I used Myrtle's phone to call the Motion Picture Stuntmen's Association to ask whether they knew of any upcoming jobs that could use my dubious talents. The individual on the switchboard named an independent television producer who needed a couple of Oriental types to do a fight scene with the hero of whatever they were shooting. I dialed the number I was given and learned that the two Japanese stuntmen already had been chosen and were doing their thing on the rental stage at that very moment. So much for that.

I thanked Myrtle and ventured out onto Hollywood

Boulevard. It was a hot day and there was little traffic moving by our normal bumper-bumping standards. The hills where the big white HOLLYWOOD sign stands were barely visible amid the summer smog. I shook my head, wondering vaguely what my horoscope said about the day. Then I took another look at the thick blanket of corrosive grayness that covered the area and knew I didn't really want to know what the rest of the day held for me.

Across the street was a bar, a sign advertising Budweiser beer winking in the otherwise darkened window. A beer would sure taste good. Then my experience of the previous night, when I felt I needed a drink after finding the body, flashed through my mind and the hair on the back of my neck stood up. I was on dangerous ground. I knew that from experience.

I found a noon meeting of Alcoholics Anonymous only four blocks away. It was held on Tuesdays and Thursdays in one of the meeting rooms of an upper-class hotel. Coffee and donuts were catered without charge, lending some credence to the rumor that the manager was an AA member himself. A collection was taken at each meeting and the loose bills and change was stuffed in an empty coffee cup by whoever was running the meeting. That was rent for the room.

I sort of expected to see someone I knew, but this day's attendees were all strangers. I sat in the back of the hall and listened to the day's speaker, a musician who once had been tops in the rhythm and blues field, his recordings selling in the millions. He admitted that somewhere along the way, booze had taken over and seemed to have eaten at his talent until there wasn't any.

"At this point, I don't even own a guitar," he announced. "I'm afraid of the re-association it might bring on." Instead, he was working in an appliance store, selling washing machines. He insisted these were the happiest days of his life, and I believed him.

Just listening to his tale and the help he had received in his efforts to recover what amounted to his sanity did something to my own emotional engine and I was feeling a lot more confident and in command of myself. When the hour-long meeting ended, I stuffed a couple of bucks in the cup. Pretty cheap peace of mind, I figured.

One of my problems lies in the fact that I have to keep busy or I start getting antsy, and that can lead to trouble. I walked back to the Heartbreak Hotel and paused in front of the coffee shop to pick up a couple of early afternoon editions, trying to ignore the sweat that ran down the back of my neck.

It was cool inside and I chose a booth where I could spread out the papers, but didn't until I had ordered a bowl of beef stew, which was listed as a specialty of the house. While I waited for it, I unfolded one of the papers to look at the front page. There were three photos reproduced there, with a blazing re-ink headline that read: *BURLESQUE QUEEN MURDERED!*

From left to right, the three one-column mug shots were of a youthful Karen Cooley, a glowering Mac

Calley, and a young, handsome Native American named Charlie Cougar.

I had no idea where they had obtained the photo of myself. It was an old head shot that had appeared in a talent directory for the film industry several years earlier. I stared at it, wondering whether I ever really had been as innocent as I appeared on the printed page.

Trying to read a newspaper and eat stew at the same time has all the makings of a minor disaster, so I pushed the papers away and concentrated on spooning vitamins into my face.

Done, I pushed the bowl away and folded the front page for easier reading. The report seemed to be based pretty much as I had told it to the police. In the story, I was listed as a process server who had found the body. The one thing I noted was that there was no mention at all of the crude and bloody crosses the tortured woman had managed to leave on the sheet. That lack of mention probably was on purpose so they could rule out the crazies who would line up to confess to the slaying.

According to an LAPD spokesman, however, it appeared that during the torture session, the woman had passed out at least once and been revived by a bucket of water thrown on her. The bedsheets close to her were still damp when the police arrived. The reporter suggested that this could help in setting the time of her death. I must really have been panicked I realized, because I had seen no evidence of dampness at the scene. But I hadn't been looking for detail, either.

The article ended by stating that due to the nature of the crime and the fear of it being the work of what could turn out to be a crazed serial killer, the normal work backlog had been put in a hold pattern at the Los Angeles County Coroner's Office. The autopsy to determine the actual cause of Karen Cooley's death would be held today.

When there are several dozen customers in cold storage vaults at the coroner's office, it can be up to a couple of weeks before the office completes its work on each and issues a report. For the police—and probably the district attorney—to arrange an autopsy so fast, there had to be some really important reason the late Miss Cooley was getting such instant attention.

I looked at the other newspaper, noting that the only photo was a posed studio shot of Karen Cooley. It was the staged type that would be used for publicity and probably blown up to one-sheet size and posted outside whatever theater in which she was taking her clothes off. This edition did mention, though, that she had retired from burlesque and had become a rather well-known makeup artist for monster movies.

This story also noted that prior to her death, the late Miss Cooley apparently had been posing as an older woman. The white wig and the way in which her face was made-up were offered as evidence. It was obvious this reporter had contacts other than the police department's public relations flack. However, there was no mention of the blood-marked sheet in this story, either. My own name was absent from this report, which was just as well.

I left the newspapers in the booth and paid my bill before passing through the swinging door to the hotel lobby.

"A message for you, Charlie," the desk clerk called to me. The fact that he could do that offers some idea as to how large the lobby really is. I crossed and he handed me a yellow slip. It was from Sam Light, and the note said he needed to see me "soonest." I called from my room and Sam's assistant put me through to him immediately.

"You've seen the afternoon editions?" he asked. I admitted I had.

"You note that the cops are holding out on the double-cross thing," he said. "I think you mentioned that you know where to find Joe Delaney."

"Yeah. He lives right next door to the Cooley place."

"How about going out there with me? I want to talk to him."

"You need a bodyguard?" I wanted to know. "I've seen Delaney up close. I don't think the two of us together could take him!"

"I don't want to fight him. I just want to talk," Light returned, his tone urgent, "but I also need a witness to verify what he might tell me. I'll even see that the newspaper pays for your time!"

Hmm. A whole new role in life for Charlie Cougar: Verifying witness. "Okay," I agreed. "How do you want to handle it?"

"I haven't been able to round up a telephone number on him yet, so that means we'll have to go out there. The cops picked him up at his home and put him through the wringer this morning and got nil. About now, they should be hauling him back to Studio City."

"Maybe." I was dubious. "If the cops put us through it and we didn't know what we know now, we'd probably ask to be let out at the nearest saloon."

"Not much chance of that. Joe Delaney doesn't drink. Never has!"

"One other thought, while you're waiting for me," Sam Light said. "You thought Karen Cooley was using her disguise to keep you from serving her a summons, right?"

"Yeah," I said slowly. "I thought that at the time."

Well, it looks like maybe she was trying to hide from someone else too. Whoever killed her was after something she had. Apparently, the disguise didn't work with him. Or her. Give it some thought."

"Why not pick me up here in front of the hotel in about thirty minutes?" I suggested.

"Done!" He hung up.

Chapter Twelve

I tried to call Sue at home, but a motherly voice told me she already had left for work. I thanked her and hung up, realizing I had made a mistake in telling Sam Light to pick me up. I could have driven to Studio City, then gone on to the bowling alley to talk to her. But on second thought, it was Wednesday night, and that was the night the steelworkers did their ball tossing. I didn't see any reason to run into them again. It's not that I'm cowardly, understand. It's just that I'm sane.

"I still have to get downtown and give the cops a statement," I told Light a few minutes later as he drove toward the San Fernando Valley.

"I wouldn't wait beyond tomorrow," he offered. "They like that sort of thing done now, if not sooner."

Sam wasn't much for talking and his features most

of the time seemed to carry a perpetual frown, as though his mind was in mortal combat with some knotty problem. I glanced at him, but said nothing.

We had met at an AA meeting some months back. At that time, he was new in town and didn't seem too involved in trying to make friends. I knew the feeling and, with us, it was a couple of loners pairing off and ignoring the rest of the world.

Over the months since, I had learned that he had been a newspaper reporter in Philadelphia after a hitch in the Marines. Later, he got called back for Desert Storm and wrote a book about the experience. No one wanted to publish it and he sort of went off the deep end, becoming a hobo for a year or so. He had become a member of Alcoholics Anonymous after losing a job as a bartender in Florida.

After hitchhiking across the country, finally he had ended up in California's Mojave Desert. He began investigating a series of multiple murders that revolved around lost treasure ships, smuggling, and stolen computer chips. Although he was an initial suspect, he had managed to report the series of homicides for a newspaper in San Francisco that was interested in the novelty of the case and its background. That had won him a job on the paper and, ultimately, the one-man operation of the paper's Los Angeles news bureau.

"What makes you think this guy Delaney is going to be at home?" I asked.

"I talked to him at the morgue. He's taking possession of the lady's body, handling a funeral. He agreed to an interview."

"That's a surprise."

Light nodded his head, keeping his eye on traffic. "Yeah. It is."

We pulled to the curb in front of the house that now was identified as belonging to Joe Delaney. The lights were on in the front of his home, making the Cooley house next to it seem drab and gray.

Delaney must have been waiting for us. Light pushed the bell just once and the door opened. We were greeted and led into a living room that looked more like a den. All of the furniture was of dark leather and there was a rolltop desk in one corner. On the other wall was a well-stocked wet bar.

"I do a lot of my work here," Delaney explained as we surveyed the room. "Fewer interruptions. Either of you care for a drink?"

"Not tonight, thanks," Light said, and I shook my head.

"What kind of work do you do now?" Sam Light asked, as he settled into one of the leather chairs to which our host had pointed. I took the one beside it. Opposite was the leather couch and Delaney eased his bulk onto that.

"I own an auto dealership in Ventura. Bought it from Mac Calley a coupla weeks before he disappeared." He paused, letting us digest that fact, then leaned forward to stare at Light.

"I know why you're here, Light, but you're not gonna hear from me the kinda dirt you expect." He was scowling and his tone was close to a growl. "Sure, Mac an' me had our times an' made good money doin' what we did, but we split up right after that movie scam came apart. I've been tryin' to play it straight, an' since he disappeared, look out for Karen." He paused for a breath adding, "And if you ask me somethin' I ain't gonna tell you, I'll tell you I ain't gonna tell you!"

He stopped then, seeming to gulp, and settled back in his chair, the scowl reduced in intensity to a frown. He turned his eyes on me.

"I remember you. You was here th' other day, lookin' straight at Karen Cooley and not knowin' who she was." He still frowned as a liquid chuckle erupted from somewhere deep in his throat. I nodded acceptance of the fact.

"You think she was all gussied up like an old lady t' fool you. She was, but you wasn't th' only one. Somebody was after her big time an' she knew it."

"Why didn't she leave town? Go somewhere to hide out?" Light wanted to know. I was feeling a bit jealous over the fact that I had been sharing her disguise with others and didn't know it. Delaney shook his head, the scowl back.

"I tried to get her to go, but she wouldn't. Said she had to stay close until her brother showed up. Wouldn't believe he's dead. Between us, we cooked up the story about her moving to Vegas, then worked out the old lady bit."

"You think Calley's dead?" Light demanded. Joe Delaney nodded again.

"He was getting ready to head for Brazil, and had cashed in everything like the auto business I got. All the bars. Even closed down the gambling. He had more'n two million bucks in cash, and he was gonna take off with it. If he'd made it to Brazil, I'd have heard from him one way or another by now. So would Karen."

"Where was he hiding the cash while he was doing all the collecting?" Light wanted to know. "If he'd put it in a safety deposit box, the Feds would know about it and would've been all over him like a tent."

Delaney shook his head. "I don't rightly know, but I have some suspicions."

"Like?" Light questioned.

"Karen. I think he gave it to her to hold till he was ready to fly. She's the only person he really trusted, and that includes me. I figger that's why she wouldn't leave her place. And that's what got her killed. It's probably what got him killed too."

"You've searched her house for it since she died?"

Hell, no!" Delaney snarled, surprised at the question. "I figger the cops've took the place apart by now and it's still sealed. I don't need a burglary rap this late in life."

"How much of this have you told the homicide people?" Light wanted to know.

"Almost all of it. I've known Karen since she was a kid, and I told Mac I'd look after her. I tried." He shook his head, eyes on his shoes. "Didn't do much good."

His head came up, face wearing a strange expression of defeat. He spread his hands and looked down at his body. "Look at me. I can't even take care of myself. I've got a bad heart. I'm diabetic. And now they think I have liver cancer. Six months left at most. What kind of a tough guy am I?"

"The other day when you came through the hedge into Karen's backyard, you had me fooled," I told him. "I thought you were tough." He ignored that, probably passing it off as false sympathy of a sort. But I had thought he was tough.

"Where were you during the time she was killed?" Light wanted to know.

That brought a grimace. "I told that to the cops too. I was at my business with my CPA, getting some quarterly taxes ready. I didn't get home till way after dark."

"Do you drive a van?" I asked. He looked at me and nodded. "I saw you pull into your driveway."

"Good. Maybe you'll tell that to the cops." It was my turn to nod.

Sam Light had been taking notes during all of this and he was looking down at them, shaking his head. "Someone besides you must have decided Karen was holding the money. Why else would she be tortured the way she was? Any idea who that might be?"

Again, Delaney shook his head. "No, but someone was fooling around in her backyard last night. Actually, about four o'clock this morning. I went out to look, but whoever it was musta heard me and run. I don't know. Maybe she talked before he killed her."

"He—or she—didn't kill her exactly," Light put in. "She died of a heart attack. Apparently, the pain was more than she could handle." He was folding up his notebook, capping his pen. No one mentioned that she possibly had not lived long enough to reveal the money's hiding place, but we all understood.

"So you're now a legitimate businessman." Light was looking Delaney up and down, judging.

"I'm trying to be." Delaney shook his head. "I know I'll never shake the old image, but I'd like to die with a little pride."

We all shook hands and Sam Light thanked him for his time.

"Thanks for not wantin' t' get into th' old days," Delaney said softly, shaking his head. "I reckon we've all had enough of that."

Back in Light's car, we sat for a moment, saying nothing. He stared down the street through the windshield, frowning. Finally he shook his head and glanced at me.

"What do you think?" he wanted to know.

"He talks like a sick old man who's afraid of where his sins are going to take him. He's probably reached the point in life where he's scared to death of the Hereafter."

Light heaved a sigh. "Maybe that's it. Then again, maybe he's after the money. I'd sure like to see his medical records."

"I saw him drive in that night," I reminded him.

"You saw somebody drive in." He started the engine and pulled into the quiet street.

"But the cops must've checked him out or he'd be in jail as a suspect," I argued. "I'm sure they must have checked the CPA for his alibi."

"Do you know who Meyer Lansky was?" He cast me an amused smile. I shook my head.

"Who's Meyer Lansky?"

"He was the bookkeeper for Al Capone back in Prohibition days. The guy who helped set up the Mafia and is given credit for creating money laundering. You think Lansky wouldn't lie for old scarface Al?"

"He probably wasn't a certified public accountant," I ventured. Light was still laughing when he dropped me off in front of the hotel. It was almost 8:00 P.M.

I had told Bob the Burglar to meet me at 6:00 P.M., but I had been so involved in listening to Joe Delaney that I had forgotten completely about Bob and my promise.

I walked through the coffee shop, looking for him, but he wasn't there. The place was almost empty, the dinner crowd was gone and only a few coffee addicts hanging in.

Heaving a sigh, I pushed through the door that led to the hotel bar, looking for him. He wasn't there either. I asked the bartender whether he had seen him.

"He was in here about six looking for you," he told me. "Don't know where he went after that."

In the lobby, I asked the college kid who was moonlighting as the desk clerk whether he had seen Bob. He shook his head, telling me he didn't know him. I had him check whether he had a room in the hotel. That was a negative too.

I was feeling a guilt that I didn't like. I had let down a man who needed me, and I was praying that he hadn't decided to chuck the whole thing and head for another bar.

I tried to imagine how I would have felt if my own sponsor had failed me that way, ignoring his promise to take me to my first meeting. Standing there, looking up and down the street, I knew, had things been reversed, I'd have cursed him up and down for leaving me hanging, then headed for the nearest bar.

But old C. D. Stilling had been there for me, and we'd made it to my first AA meeting. Stilling was a legend on the rodeo circuit as a trick rider, his specialty being to ride two horses, a booted foot on the back of each, as he jumped them over a Buick convertible.

He was a real crowd pleaser at what he did and no one who knew him could figure out how he accomplished it. After each jump, he would race the two horses around the arena, tipping his hat to the crowd before he made his exit. In back of the bucking chutes and out of sight of the audience, he would fall between the horses, dead drunk and out cold.

Stilling later told me he drank because he was afraid of the act and needed the false courage. Eventually, the fear took over even when he was drunk. He almost died when he and the two horses ended up in the backseat of the convertible during one show. The two horses, both with broken legs, were put down, and Stilling was hauled off to the hospital. He joined Alcoholics Anonymous and began training jumping horses for teenage girls. Later, he started furnishing bucking horses to rodeos as a stock contractor.

Still standing on the curb, oblivious to the passing traffic, I knew I was no C. D. Stilling. I was still thinking that when I let myself into my room and turned on the light.

Bob the Burglar was asleep on my bed. At first, I wanted to grab him and throw him out the window, then I paused to realize he had needed a place to wait for me. For him, getting into my room would have been no problem at all. And if he was there to steal something, he wouldn't have stayed.

I bent over him, listening to his quiet snoring, smelling his exhaled breath. It was pretty rank, but he hadn't been drinking.

Deciding not to wake him, I glanced at the room's one rickety chair and knew it wouldn't make much of a bed. Instead, I opened the closet and pulled out my old saddle and the dry-cleaned saddle blankets. Stripping down to my shorts, I unfolded the blankets, lay down, and pulled them over me, settling my head on the seat of the saddle.

I hadn't slept like this since my last roundup on the reservation at the age of sixteen. With that single recollection, I knew it wasn't going to be comfortable, but I figured I owed Bob something, if only a decent night's sleep.

Chapter Thirteen

Bob the Burglar was gone when I managed to sit up the next morning. In spite of a stiff neck, I had slept like the dead. I guess the relief at finding Bob had not gone off on a drunk had allowed me to relax beyond my usual level. He had left a note, apologizing for the break-in, adding that he had to get to work and would see me later.

I was in the middle of shaving when the phone rang.

"Do you still work here?" Danny Dark wanted to know.

"I'm not really sure," I told him, doing my best to make my tone as disgusted as his. "My last job turned out to be less than profitable."

"Yeah, I know." His tone softened a bit. "But I'm going to make it up to you. I have four or five easy

114

ones and they're all yours. How soon can you come in?"

"I have to go down to the cop shop and give them a statement first thing," I told him. "I'll be there early this afternoon."

"Okay. I'll expect you." There was a pause. "Where've you been hiding out? I tried to reach you yesterday and again last night."

"You didn't leave a message." He never did. "I've been doing some work for a newspaper guy. He's paying me by the hour."

"Well, right now, I need you more than he does. Serve this stuff and you'll have money to jingle in your jeans."

"This afternoon," I promised.

In Los Angeles, if you want to live, you keep your eyes on the road when driving. The safest attitude is that every other driver is looking for a chance to kill you. The evening before, with Sam Light doing the driving, I'd had a chance to see all sorts of new buildings and businesses I'd been missing. That was one of the reasons I decided to take a bus downtown to Parker Center, the hub of LAPD activities.

It was a warm, breezy California morning and I enjoyed the trip, since there were only a few passengers and we passed a lot of standard stops. Walking from the bus stop to the center, I noted that the downtown area hadn't changed much since the last time I had looked.

It took me a couple of hours to write out my version

of what I had done and seen in Karen Cooley's house the night of her death. Since I had seen no mention in any news stories or telecasts, I made a point of mentioning the blood-marked pair of crosses I had noted on the bedsheet beside her body.

When done, I went to a dispenser and bought a cup of coffee while the report was typed for my signature. When the smooth copy came back, I read it, then signed it and was asked to wait again, while copies were made. I left with one copy tucked in my hip pocket.

On the bus back to Hollywood, I reread my statement. Everything was exactly as I had written it. I couldn't think of anything I had left out.

I got off and wandered into the lobby to check my messages. Nothing. About then, I realized I'd had no breakfast, so I passed through the door into the coffee shop. It was almost noon.

The daily special was Salisbury steak with mashed potatoes, gravy and mixed vegetables, coffee on the side. I went for it and wolfed it down before I headed for Dark's office.

He had the legal papers ready and handed three sets to me. One was for a local court bailiff whose wife was filing for divorce in Orange County. I figured I could catch him at the courthouse. He wouldn't like it, of course, but I didn't want to chase him all over town. The other two should be equally as simple to serve.

"I'll be back tomorrow to get paid on these," I promised Dark and turned toward the door.

"You've got something hanging out of your back pocket," he announced. I reached for it, realizing it was my statement for the cops.

"Yeah. A copy of what I wrote at Parker Center," I told him.

"Sounds interesting." He extended his hand. "Can I read it?"

I started to refuse, but there was no reason I could think of. I handed it to him and he unfolded it. I poured a cup of coffee while he digested the prose.

He finally folded the report and handed it back, shaking his head thoughtfully. "Sounds like a real mess. Sorry it was you there, but I'm happy it wasn't me."

I had a sudden thought. "What kind of an operation was it that would cost her fifty grand?"

Dark nodded. "Pretty complicated, I guess. She came down sick and they thought she had a separated aorta. For that, they cut her from her wishbone clear down to her navel. Then they found that wasn't the problem. Instead, she had a growth—a tumor, I was told—that was starting to encircle her heart. They had to take the heart clear out of the body in order to remove the tumor. Then they put the heart back in place and sewed her up."

I shook my head. "Sounds like a deal for the price at today's hospital costs. The last time I was in one, it cost me four bucks for a Band-Aid."

"Cooley didn't think so. She filed suit against the hospital for ruining her career as a stripper, claiming medical malpractice. She couldn't expose much bare skin, I guess, if she had a scar the full length of her belly. Actually, though, they probably saved her life. The judge threw her claim out of court, so she just refused to pay the hospital."

"She never appeared on a stage again?

Dark shook his head. "Not so far as I know. That's when she went into the makeup field and finally ended up creating stuff for those monster films." He glanced at his watch. "Not that I'm trying to rush you, but if you want to get paid tomorrow, you'd best get moving."

I called Sue Tallfeather and caught her at home before she headed for one of her classes. She said she was working that night, and when I asked, had no objections to my stopping by later and having a cup of coffee with her.

"I expected to hear from you before this," she said. "What did you do after you took me home? Go back to that house and go in?"

"Yeah," I admitted. "I did that."

"It's scary. From what I read in the papers, we could have been cruising past her house at the time the murder was going on."

"I guess that's possible."

"See. I keep you out of trouble," she announced. "If I hadn't been along, you'd have gone in then and probably gotten stabbed or shot like her dog was."

"I agree, honey. You're a real lifesaver in more ways than one."

"Charlie, sometimes I don't know what you're talking about, but you can explain it all tonight. I have to run."

During the afternoon, I ran down two of the folks someone wanted to drag into court. The bailiff was a little upset that I'd collared him in the courtroom, but I waited until the judge had called a recess and no one but the bailiff was present. If he was embarrassed, he shouldn't have been. I try not to make enemies unless it becomes a necessity. The plain truth is that nobody loves a process server. The second service was to a woman attorney who was being sued for malpractice. I caught her in her office. The third guy, buyer for a pharmacy chain, turned out to be at a trade show in Toledo. I'd have to wait until he returned.

I called Dark's office, but he was out. Myrtle took the call. I told her which of the subjects I had served and for Dark to have a check ready in the morning. I'd be by.

It was almost 6:00 P.M., so I went back to the hotel, where I bought an afternoon edition, then showered and changed.

The paper carried a syndicated article by Sam Light that covered our meeting with Joe Delaney. The story was owned by the paper in San Francisco for which Sam worked and apparently was considered interesting enough that they had put it out through their network to other buyers. At least, that's the way the operation had been explained to me.

I was surprised at the tack taken by Light. When we left the house the previous night, he had seemed suspicious of Delaney. But in the news feature, he tended to paint him as a man who knew he was dying and was attempting to set himself straight with society.

In fact, Light made Delaney sound semiheroic, serving as Karen Cooley's protector over the years, maybe even standing between her and her wild brother. He also made the point that Delaney was feeling deep guilt over the fact that he had not been on hand to prevent her murder.

What followed, though, was a short outline regarding some of Delaney's more doubtful activities over the years, some of them connected with the missing Mac Calley. He also mentioned that Delaney had been convicted of two felonies over the years. Delaney wasn't going to like that part of the article, I figured, but the contrast in old and more recent behavior helped to better establish the feelings of pain and guilt expressed in the earlier paragraphs. But who am I to judge?

A last paragraph stated that a funeral service for the late Karen Alice Calley would be held at a Catholic church in East Los Angeles the next morning at 10 A.M. That would be Friday. It would be a closed casket service.

I was just turning to the sports section when my phone rang. It was Sam Light. "See my story?" he wanted to know.

Just finished it. Nice job. What changed your mind about Delaney being involved?"

"He's not off the hook, but almost," came the reply. "Joe gave the cops permission to contact his doctor. The doc verifies everything we were told last night.

Said Joe probably has more like three months to live rather than six."

"And it stands to reason a dying man is not going to carve up an old friend just to locate a couple of million dollars," I added. "That your reasoning?"

"Right. I'm going to the funeral in the morning. Why don't you come with me?"

"Am I on the payroll for that?" I asked, then felt guilty for asking. After all, I'd found the lady. To attend would be common decency. "Forget I asked that."

"No. I'm on the payroll, so you are, too. That's the way it works."

We made arrangements to meet outside the church. That way, I could go from there to Danny Dark's office and collect my loot. He might have a couple of more things for me to serve by then.

I was hungry and took the elevator down, checking the desk for messages. Nothing. As I entered the coffee shop, I saw Bob the Burglar in one of the booths, staring at the menu.

"Mind if I slide in here?" I asked.

He looked up, grinning. He was bright-eyed and sober, which made me feel better about the earlier foul-up. "Be my guest," he said.

I took a seat and faced him. "Look, I apologize for what happened the other night. All my fault. How about tonight? Want to make a meeting?" I'd have plenty of time for that before I saw Sue. She'd be done at the bowling alley around 11:00 P.M., she'd told me. Bob shook his head.

"Can't. Got another night shoot starting at eight. They're paying top bucks for night work."

"How about tomorrow night? Friday?"

He considered for a moment, frowning, then nodded. "I'll meet you here. What time?"

"Meeting starts at eight. It's in the basement of that church up on Yucca Street. We can walk from here. Let's make it seven o'clock."

Bob agreed and we both settled on liver and onions when the waitress came around. It was the evening's cheapest special, which I'm sure told us something about each other. We were both short of cash—or expected to be. That's a standard Hollywood syndrome. Done eating, Bob went to work and I sat in the booth, pondering what I was going to do before I met Sue.

Sam Light had given me that envelope full of clipping copies about Joe Delaney. That no doubt was where he had learned about the old hood's earlier runins with the law. They were up in my room and I decided to look at them. It would pass a little time.

I spread the stuff out on the round table that seems standard for most hotel rooms and started to sort it out by date. Then I stopped. I had come across the reproduction of the news photo I had seen earlier of Mac Calley about to get into a vehicle while the man I now knew was Joe Delaney was holding the door open.

However, Mac Calley was looking over the top of the car. On the other side of the vehicle was something I had missed the first time I looked at the picture. Standing there, scowling at Calley, was a man I knew well. One Danny Dark!

Chapter Fourteen

"I've seen what's down on Main Street, Charlie. I've seen what happens to a lot of our people who try to drink. My grandparents don't drink. My parents don't. And I got the lectures from all of them from the time I could understand." Sue Tallfeather was glaring at me.

Los Angeles' Main Street is the street of lost dreams, peopled by the homeless, the mentally damaged, and the alcoholics. It has been that way for as long as anyone can remember and, apparently, the city is willing to let it stay that way as long as the helpless don't venture any farther. Actually, it's no different than any other place. Show me a city, even a town, and I'll show you its skid row. I'd been on several of them, but I was surprised that Sue Tallfeather had been exposed, even as a tourist.

We had ended up in an all-night place that had a bar not far from the bowling alley. Like all the other liquor-serving establishments in the state of California, it had to close down that part of the operation at 2:00 A.M. I had told Sue I was having coffee, then asked if she would prefer a drink. She looked a little frazzled after eight hours or so of putting up with all-male bowling leagues.

"Don't get upset," I told her. "I just made an offer."

"I think you're testing me," she charged, scowling. "You want to know whether I drink and, if I do, whether I can handle it."

"I was trying to be a gentleman," I told her. Truth is, I *was* testing her. I'd had experience with women who drank too much.

"What does your Alcoholics Anonymous say about Indians and drinking?" she wanted to know. Her scowl had subsided to a frown. I had to shrug.

"There are all sorts of theories, but the truth is that we're no different than other people in the rest of the world. Some Indians just can't handle booze."

"What do you think?"

I offered a shrug. "I don't know. Boredom. There's not much to do on some of the reservations. I'm sure that's one of the reasons your family got out of the Dakotas."

"No opportunity," she agreed. "My grandfather told me once he didn't really want to live in the white man's world, but he didn't want his wife and children to live in poverty, either. That's why he came to California and got a defense job during World War Two."

The waitress took our order for black coffee and recited the dessert menu. Sue decided to have a piece of apple pie. When we were alone again, it seemed we had reached some sort of truce about my supposedly subtle prying.

I told her about Bob the Burglar and how he needed help and how I had screwed up with him. She was satisfied, though, with the announcement that I was taking him to a meeting the next night. Then she suddenly frowned.

"Tomorrow's Friday," she pointed out. "It's also the last day of the month. Don't most of the studios pay tomorrow?

I knew in that moment why Bob had hesitated before he agreed to meet me for the meeting. He had been thinking the same thing. I shrugged, not looking at her. "Not much I can do at this point. If he's going to party, he's going to party."

"I hope not." Our coffee and the thin slice of pie had arrived. I raised my cup for a sip, as she used her fork to cut off a small piece of pie.

"The pie okay?"

"Not bad. Better than I expected." She glanced at the clock on the wall that was within our line of vision. "It's coming up one o'clock, and I have to be in class at nine."

It was truth time, I decided. We were staring into each other's eyes when I told her, "Sue, I *was* testing you when I asked whether you wanted a drink. I guess it was subconscious, but what you said made me realize that's what I was doing."

She said nothing, just stared and I wasn't certain how to proceed. I just bulled into it. "I think you're the finest lady I've ever run into, and I want our relationship to grow into something bigger and better than a cup of coffee after work. I want to spend more time with you. We need to get to know each other. That's what I want."

I looked down at the tabletop, hoping she wouldn't laugh. Instead, her hand came across to rest on top of mine. "I want that too, Charlie, but there are problems."

I looked up and there was sadness in her expression. "I'm afraid of getting too close to you, Charlie. What kind of future do you have, running after people to get them into a courtroom? That's trading on other people's misfortunes. If it's not that, you're falling off of horses, off buildings, or down staircases. How long can you do that before it catches up? What kind of future are you planning for yourself? What would be the future for me?"

There was nothing I could say. She was talking about a way of life I understood. Maybe I didn't always like it, but I did understand what I was doing, how to do it, whether it was chasing people or falling horses. I didn't know much else. I stared into her eyes for a long moment, then shook my head, eyes going back to the table.

"I don't know," I told her. "I guess I haven't ever looked much beyond tomorrow. I know you want more than that."

She nodded. "Yes, I do." She slid out of the booth

and I stood up too. "If I'm going to make it to school on time, I have to go."

She had followed me from the bowling alley in her own car. I left enough cash on the table to include a respectable tip and took her arm, guiding her toward the door. In the parking lot, she handed me her keys and I opened the door for her, checking the backseat to be sure she didn't have any unwanted passengers. You learn to do that sort of thing in Southern California these days.

"I'm sorry, Charlie," she said softly, turning toward me, putting a hand on my shoulder. "I had to tell you the truth about how I feel. Please give some thought to what I said."

I nodded. "I will. You know that." That was when I bent to kiss her and felt the electricity running through my system. I wondered if it was having the same effect on her. There was something powerful between us. That's the only way I could describe it. Finally, she drew away, smiling at me.

"That was nice, Charlie." I tried to pull her closer, but she shook her head, still smiling.

"Let's do that some more," I breathed.

"Not tonight. We'll be talking some more."

"How about another trip up to the lake?" I offered, and she nodded.

"It was nice up there." The car door was standing open and she twisted away from me and slipped onto the seat. "Say good night, Charlie Cougar."

"Good night, Sue Tallfeather."

It all seemed a little formal and I felt a pang of

doubt as she closed the door, started the motor, and pulled away. I stood there, wishing she'd come back, knowing she wouldn't. Not after the things she had said to me.

As I drove back to Hollywood, I was reviewing what had passed between us. My stoic facade was shot to pieces with her and I chuckled at the thought. I had never talked to anyone the way I had her. Also, I realized, there had been nothing in the way of real commitment in the things I had said.

I shook my head as I turned onto the freeway off-ramp. I tried to tell myself the idea of Charlie Cougar wanting to marry an Indian who didn't know her heritage was downright ridiculous. Wait until I told her how courtship was conducted among the Apaches.

For the most part, I had been brought up to believe that young Apache girls seeking husbands did the choosing. When she finally decided on one, she came into his lodge and prepared his breakfast each morning before sending him off. This went on for about a week before she returned to her parents' home, be it a house or a tipi. If the brave was interested enough to want her as a wife, he then had to deal with her father as to how many horses he would have to give the old man. If it didn't work out later, divorce was simple. One or the other just moved out.

I laughed outright. I'd have to ask her what kind of horses her father liked. Even better, I could haul one down and stake it out on his front lawn. After all, the Sioux and Apaches had some things in common. With both, horses were the common currency when it came to acquiring a bride!

At the hotel, there was a yellow message slip in my mail slot. There had been a call from Sam Light, reminding me about a meeting at the church the next morning. He wanted to meet at about 9:15 so we would have time to talk before Karen Cooley's funeral. I left a wake-up call with the desk clerk for 6:30 A.M.

The bar was empty and the night bartender was cleaning things up. I asked whether he had seen Bob the Burglar. He hadn't. It looked like Bob was still holding fast. But it was already Friday, the danger day.

I went up to my room and made it to bed, but I couldn't sleep. I was thinking about the things Sue Tallfeather had said. Down underneath, I had known for some time that I was going to have to change my way of life. Like Sue had mentioned, you can't fall on your head forever. It's generally agreed that the useful professional life of a stuntman is about five years. Some go on a lot longer than that but you could either end up dead or permanently impaired in the Motion Picture Country Home and Hospital. The smart ones graduated to second units directing action sequences or they became stunt coordinators. These jobs involved setting up the stunts and telling others how they are to be done instead of doing the fall.

The one possible exception—a legend in his day— was a second-unit director named Breezy Eason. Back in the thirties, he'd wanted Warner Brothers' singing cowboy, Dick Foran, to ride his horse down a steep trail. Foran, a product of the Ivy League colleges, wasn't so enthusiastic and demanded that Eason show him how.

The director, showing his disgust, got on a horse and spurred it over the edge. The horse fell and they went tumbling down the face of what amounted to a minor cliff. Luckily, somewhere along the way, animal and rider parted company. When they reached bottom, Eason got up and looked up the cliff to the actor. "That's the way it's done," he declared. "Now do it!" Foran demanded a professional stuntman. They say that was the last stunt Breezy Eason ever tried.

As for being a process server, I guess I felt that was a little like being a warrior. I was able to use my brains, wits, and other faculties to stalk what amounted to my enemy. In touching him, I was counting coup, as the old warriors called it; getting close enough to an enemy to touch him.

One thing I hadn't told Sue about AA was that their original theory and the one still followed is that all alcoholics are emotionally immature. How could I explain my feelings about what I did without her wanting me to check into the psycho ward of the same Motion Picture Country Home and Hospital where some of my friends were passing their days?

I finally sat up in bed and reached over to the small radio that I kept on a stand within reach. I turned the dial to an all-night station that offered soft, soothing music without getting too classical. Other times, late at night, I found that the soft sounds helped to untie some of my tension.

I was on the point of dozing off when a news flash flayed me back to consciousness.

"If you live in Studio City and see a man wearing a Wolf Man's mask creeping through your backyard, dial 911 immediately. This is not a joke!" the measured baritone announced.

"One man is dead and another is being sought by police after they found the two inside the house where exotic dancer Karen Cooley was slain several days ago. According to a police spokesperson, the two men were systematically wrecking the interior of the house, having destroyed several walls.

"A concerned neighbor reportedly called the police when he heard sounds of destruction coming from the Cooley property. When the Los Angeles police arrived, one suspect, who was wearing the mask of a werewolf, fled. The other suspect was surrounded and, reportedly armed, was about to fire at officers when he was shot. He was pronounced dead at the scene. Thus far, no identification of the dead man has been released by the police department.

"Officers are being close-mouthed about the reason for the break-in but the popular theory, according to reporters, is that the two suspects were searching for the two million dollars that racketeer Mac Calley allegedly had in his possession at the time of his disappearance. Calley is Karen Cooley's brother."

The newscaster identified himself, promising later bulletins. I sat up and turned off the radio. It had to have been Joe Delaney who called the cops. The comment about the search for the two million might also have come from him.

But a burglar wearing a werewolf's mask? Give me a break!

Chapter Fifteen

"**D**id you hear that report last night about the werewolf tearing up Karen Cooley's house?" I asked. "He got away, while his partner tried to stand off the cops?"

Sam Light shook his head, watching several people drifting toward us from the parking lot. "I didn't hear that bulletin, but I checked it all out and got the real scoop at the cop shop this morning. The cops didn't shoot the guy. He was about to surrender, when the werewolf, apparently hiding in the bushes, took him out. He had a car in the alley and took off before the cops could do anything."

"You're kidding!"

"I'm not. There were four cops, two patrolmen and a backup team. When they spotted the guy in the werewolf costume, he was running from them, but the other man was facing them with a pistol. They yelled for both of them to surrender. The guy closest to them dropped his gun and raised his hands. Just before he dived into the bushes, the werewolf turned and took him out with a silenced pistol. They figure it's the same silenced gun that was used to kill Cooley's dog. Somehow, that radio report you heard got garbled."

We were standing in front of the church where Karen Alice Cooley's funeral was to take place. I had arrived only moments earlier to find Light already there. With a look of disgust, he was watching as a television van pulled up, blocking access to the sidewalk. Several technicians with video cameras and sound equipment had dismounted, setting up shop halfway up the walkway to the church.

Getting out of the van was the anchor for one of the local stations. With his seventy-five-dollar haircut and a carefully groomed mustache, he checked his facial appearance in the van's side mirror, then turned to walk up in front of the camera. I recognized his face, but I never had bothered to learn his name.

He looked at Light, grinning. "Good morning, Sam. Mind if I interview you on the air? Might be good for your image."

"Is this going to be a live broadcast?" Light asked with cold politeness.

"That it is," the anchor enthused. "News as it happens."

"Sure. You can put me in front of your camera," Sam agreed, expression suddenly growing hard. Then he muttered something that only the anchor men could hear.

"Wait a minute, Light," the other started, but Sam shook his head and turned away, muttering, "Vultures!"

Together we walked up to the entrance to the church, pausing to look back as voices were raised. A black Lincoln had just drawn up to the curb. One well-tailored man got out of the front seat and opened the rear door, standing back as Joe Delaney came out. Another man slid out behind him.

The three conferred in low tones at the curb, Delaney apparently issuing orders, the others nodding their understanding. Meantime, the anchor had charged down upon them. Microphone in hand, he jammed it in front of Delaney, trying to block his way. The old hood glared at him as he shook his head, elbowing past. One of the bodyguards stepped in front of Delaney to run interference, while the other man protected him from the side on which the microphone was being jabbed at him like a fencing foil. At one point, the mike was directly in front of the bodyguard. An arm lashed out, knocking the instrument from the anchor's hands. It shattered on the brick walkway. The anchor stared down at the pieces in disbelief.

Delaney saw us at the entrance to the church as he climbed the brick steps and paused, looking at Light.

"Sorry we all have to be here, Joe," Light said to him softly. Delaney stared at him for a moment, then nodded, almost smiling.

"Come see me after the burial," he growled, then

marched through the open doors to the church, a bodyguard on each side. Light and I followed them in and
slid onto the polished wood of the last pew.

Delaney paused and motioned to seats for his bodyguards. They looked about suspiciously, then lowered
themselves onto the edges of the pew. Delaney continued down the carpet to the rosewood casket that
stood at the front of the church. Fumbling in his coat
pocket, he drew out something brightly metallic that
looked like a necklace or a chain. I still couldn't see
it clearly, as he laid it on the top of the casket, then
used both hands to carefully arrange it in what appeared to be a circle.

Stepping back, Delaney surveyed his work, then
crossed himself and took a seat in the front row.
Slowly others began to file into the church, and from
where we sat, I had the chance to look them over. A
few of them, women in their forties, I guessed, arrived
as a group and moved into pews about half-way to the
front. I had noted the makeup was overdone on several
of them, as well as their dress, which I questioned as
being appropriate for a funeral.

"Retired strippers," Light whispered to me. "They
used to work with her, I expect."

There were a number of couples I took to be her
neighbors or friends from Studio City, and a contin-
gent of perhaps a dozen men who seemed to be carbon
copies of Joe Delaney in general appearance, mode of
dress, and demeanor. They passed us and settled into
pews behind the oddly clad women.

"They look like old gangsters," I suggested in a stage whisper. Light nodded.

"Some're members of Calley's old gang. Maybe all of them. I understand they claim they are retired businessmen."

I looked at him. "You mean hoods can retire?" All that brought was a shrug, because Light had turned to look at the open door behind us, suddenly scowling. I turned also, to find Danny Dark standing there, seeming uncertain as to what his next move should be. He saw us staring at him and inclined his head slightly in acknowledgment of our presence. Then he marched down the carpet and took a seat by himself on the opposite side of the aisle. He sat there, no one near him, staring straight ahead at the coffin.

Organ music began to fill the church, although I couldn't see the organist. He probably was hidden somewhere amid the impressive array of organ pipes that reached halfway to the arched ceiling. After several pieces, a young priest entered and introduced himself, saying he never had the opportunity to know Karen Alice Cooley, but he was certain that she was not so different from the rest of us when it came to ambitions, fears, and facing death.

The young priest certainly had not known the lady now encased by rosewood, although he did his best to make her seem like a wholesome, God-fearing individual. He couldn't say any more than that.

Finally it was over, and the organ took up the silence again as the pall bearers appeared and began to wheel the coffin up the aisle toward the front of the church. We all rose and faced the aisle, waiting for it to pass.

Bending forward into the aisle, I had a closer look at the chain Joe Delaney had arranged atop the coffin lid. It was of heavy silver and at the bottom of it was a cross that appeared to be fashioned from silver tubing. What would serve as the upright was about four inches long. The tubing was perhaps a quarter-inch in diameter and sealed on each end. The cross arm was made of silver that was slightly smaller in diameter, shorter in length and also was closed on the ends.

I looked up to see Danny Dark staring at the same religious device. Then it was gone, being loaded into the waiting hearse that had been backed onto the brick walkway. The television crew was still present, but somewhat subdued. The obnoxious anchor was nowhere in sight.

People started filing out of the church. Sam Light and I ended up on the steps in front, watching the doors being closed on the hearse. That was when someone paused beside me and I glanced over to see that it was Danny Dark.

"I didn't expect to see you here," I told him. He cast me a glance that was supposed to freeze me.

"I'm paying my respects to an old associate. Karen and I worked together at Metropolitan," he announced. "I was studio production manager and was involved in a couple of those monster pictures on which she handled the makeup." I took that in, wondering what he had done wrong to go from studio executive to freelance second unit director. Something for sure.

"How well did you know her?" Sam Light wanted to know, suddenly interested. Dark shook his head, looking back to the street as the hearse pulled away.

"We were never bosom buddies or anything like that. We just worked together and I respected her craft. I think she respected what I did too." There was an instant's pause. "At least I hope so."

"I don't mean to be crass at a moment like this," I told him, "but it would save me a trip to your office if you happened to have my check in your pocket."

He gave me another of those chilling looks, then shook his head. "I didn't expect to see you here, either."

"It reached the point that I started to feel like I knew the lady. Like you, I'm paying my respects," I told him. "Are you going to the cemetery or back to your office?"

"The office. Come there and I'll pay you for the two services you made. I have a couple more easy ones for you too."

"I'll be along," I told him as he raised a hand and walked slowly down the steps, heading toward the parking lot.

"A strange little man," Light mused, looking after him. "I wonder what he did before he got in the movie business."

"I have no idea, but I did notice something you maybe missed. That silver cross Joe put on the casket is an almost exact miniature of the clothesline poles in Karen Cooley's backyard. Even to the little metal caps to cover the open ends."

"I knew there was something stirring my subconscious," Light admitted, "but I didn't hook into it. I wonder how Joe came by the piece."

"He invited you to visit," I reminded. "In spite of all the aging gangsters I saw in there, I think he's a lonely old man. They didn't seem to pay much attention to him."

Light glanced back into the church. "I didn't see him or the bodyguards come out. Their driver must've picked them up at a back door." He shook his head. "I'd better get back to the office and write this up. Not much to report, actually. Maybe I'll try to get with Joe tonight and find out more about what's going on."

True to his promise, Danny Dark was in his office when I walked in shortly after noon. I had parked at the hotel and walked the several blocks to his place. And all the time I was walking, I was trying to recall something I had meant to mention to Sam Light. Something important, I had thought. But now it was gone. There were so many unconnected facts and fictions involved in the Cooley/Calley thing that I was no longer able to keep track. It was getting to be like Abbott and Costello's old "Who's On First?" vaudeville routine.

Dark handed me the check and three more sets of court papers, and I glanced at the first one. It was for a housewife, who was way over the limit on her credit card—by about $15,000—and wasn't making any effort to pay. Her defense was that she had not asked for the card. It had simply arrived in the mail.

Dark had been watching me. "You could probably

catch that first one at home tonight," he suggested, then added, "unless she has a new credit card."

I gave him the laugh he expected and was starting for the door when his voice stopped me.

"What was that chain and cross thing on the coffin?" he wanted to know. I glanced over my shoulder at him and he was shaking his head. "I've never seen anything like that at a funeral before. In an open-coffin deal, the corpse may be holding a rosary or have a cross and chain around the neck, but not this!" His tone was a trifle irritated and I shook my head.

"All I know is that Joe Delaney showed up early with his two bodyguards and walked up to the coffin. He had it in his coat pocket and arranged it on the coffin lid." The comment on my explanation was a dissatisfied growl accompanied by a dismissing wave of the hand.

With no breakfast and no lunch, it was time to treat the inner man. I headed for the hotel coffee shop, wondering what the special was. But I did stop at my bank along the way to deposit Dark's check and to draw some walking-around money for my wallet.

I figured I could catch the housewife right after dinner and serve her the summons. No telling whether her husband knew about the situation, but that was not my problem.

After that, I could call Sue at the bowling alley and see whether she wanted to do another coffee and pie night. I'd had time to think about her fears and wants, and she'd had time to think about my own.

I had lunch and went up to my room for a nap. After the radio announcement about the masked burglar, there hadn't been much sleep the previous night.

It was after six when I awoke to the blaring of auto horns. I sat up and looked out the window to Hollywood Boulevard. At the intersection, two late-model cars had collided and the owners were standing in the street, shaking their fists at each other. Traffic was blocked from all four corners, and drivers eager to get home after a hard day in the corporate salt mines were standing on their horns. Welcome to L.A. quitting time, otherwise known as the six o'clock follies.

I splashed some water on my face and combed my hair, figuring I'd look respectable for the service. Dark had suggested the dinner hour, so I would wait until later for dinner. Maybe before I went to the bowling alley to pick up Sue. On that note, I called her.

She was already at work, of course, and someone had to call her to the phone. I asked about seeing her later and she begged off, saying she had to study for a test the next day.

"You start studying at midnight?" I asked.

"When I have to," she answered, a scolding note in her tone, "and I'm not supposed to take personal calls here."

"How about I stop there and maybe you can take a break for a cup of your bartender's coffee?"

There was hesitation, then a tone of disturbed surrender, as she said, "Okay. Stop by. I have to go now." I wondered if she had any idea how much I wanted to see her. I wanted to hold her and exchange kisses. But I'd settle for simply looking at her.

"Cougar," I told myself aloud, "you are in deep trouble. Twenty-seven years old and you've never felt this way before. Dangerous!"

The housewife lived in Glendale, and I learned later that her husband had learned about the debt and walked. She was having dinner with two young children when I knocked. She opened the door and I handed her the summons.

"What's this?" she demanded. She was in her early forties, I figured, and looked ten years older. She wore thick glasses and her hair was dyed a shade of red that she must have concocted herself. It couldn't have come out of a standard commercial bottle.

"A court summons," I said, knowing where this was going.

"How could you?" she demanded, throwing the papers back at me and bursting into tears. I stepped back, allowing the papers to fall to her front steps.

"No, ma'am. The question is: How could you? You have been duly served and I'd show up in court. As a friendly tip, I wouldn't open my front door anymore until I knew who was calling. It's dangerous."

Back in my car, I found a Denny's restaurant and had dinner. It was standard fast-food fare, but filling. It was going on 9:00 P.M. I hoped Sue was having a slow night as I drove in her direction, catching the Hollywood Freeway.

It was a warm night and I had the windows down, preferring real air to air-conditioning. I was in the right lane when I found that a car was pacing me on the left. I didn't pay much attention at first, but finally turned to glance at the other driver.

I was staring into the snarling face of a werewolf! And said creature had an automatic pistol with a silencer pointed at me. He fired an instant after I slammed on the brakes and began to skid. Two of my wheels caught the curb of an off-ramp, and the vehicle was literally jerked off the freeway. During this wild moment, I noted that the bullet had dug a gash across the exterior of my windshield.

I heard something break beneath the vehicle and the brakes suddenly were gone. All I could do was hang on to the wheel and hope seat belts really worked!

Chapter Sixteen

Thankfully, the off-ramp was a long, gentle curve to a stoplight at the bottom. With no foot-activated brakes, I was able to use the emergency release handle to slow my speed, however jerky it might be. I was in a residential area and most of the citizens had made it home before my abrupt arrival. Alone on the ramp, I was able to further reduce speed by shifting down to low with a clattering of gears.

In those seconds, there was too much adrenaline flowing for me to feel fear, but I did keep checking my rearview mirror to determine whether the werewolf had circled and was coming back.

The light at the bottom of the ramp was green, and I was lucky enough to wheel across the intersecting street and directly into a residential driveway. Using the emergency break, I came to a stop behind an aging van. No sooner had I turned off the engine than lights came on and a large man with a beer can in his hand appeared in the doorway.

"Some problem, mister?" he called, as I got out of the machine. I was eyeing the crease across my windshield, realizing that had I not braked as violently as I had, the bullet probably would have found its mark.

"Sorry to litter up your property," I told him, "but a drive-by shooter just tried to take me out. Can I use your phone to call the police?"

"Sure! Sure! Come on in." He pointed to his door with the beer can, as I turned off the headlights and slid between the bumpers of his van and my machine.

Inside, the house was small and cozy with furnishings that probably had been handed down through several generations. He pointed to a yellow telephone on a desk, as he said, "I was lucky this time. I've lost four cars to people who've had brakes fail and come off that ramp out of control."

I nodded understanding, then glanced at him. "With your permission, I'd like to make three calls. One of them's a toll call, but I'll pay you for it."

"Shucks!" he waved the beer can at me. "Go ahead, so long as it ain't Timbuktu!"

I dialed Sam Light's apartment number and woke him. I didn't wait for him to get fully awake. I figured my news would take care of that.

"Sam, this is Charlie. Our werewolf just tried to take me out. Bullet hit my windshield. I managed to make it to an off-ramp but then my brakes went out."

"Are you okay? Not hurt?" He was awake.

"I'm okay, but I have to call the cops. I think maybe you ought to be out here."

"Color me there!" he declared. I gave him the address and hung up.

"That the same werewolf the cops were chasing the other night?" my host wanted to know. He was in his sixties and perhaps a little bleary-eyed from an evening of solo beer-drinking. Maybe six feet tall, he was graying, but still had good muscle tone in his suntanned face. I knew him from somewhere.

"You're a horse wrangler, aren't you?" I asked as I dialed 911. He nodded, starting to speak, but I held up my hand as the phone was answered. I told the operator what had happened, then repeated the address. I was told to stand by until a patrol car arrived.

"How'd you know I was a wrangler?" the man wanted to know. "Harry Coats. Been at it for thirty years."

"I'm Charlie Cougar," I told him. "We worked together once, I think."

He nodded. "Hollywood's a small town. Or it used to be."

I dialed again. This time it was the bowling alley. Sue was serving, so I had to wait, grinning at Harry Coats.

"How about a beer, Charlie?" he offered. I shook my head.

"Not if I'm going to be talking to the cops," I told him and he nodded, understanding.

"Charlie, I asked you not to call me here!" Sue Tallfeather's tone was a bit sharp, but not as bad as I had expected it to be.

"Sorry. I figured this was an emergency of sorts."

Her tone was suddenly concerned. "What kind of emergency? What's wrong?"

"My brakes went out and I think I took out a highway sign while I was trying to get to the off-ramp," I explained.

"Are you hurt? Tell me!"

"I'm okay, but I don't think I'm going to be able to join you there. I have to call a tow truck and I probably should tell the highway patrol about their sign. I just wanted you to know you aren't being stood up deliberately by your favorite Apache."

"Charlie. You're impossible!" She giggled, then she was serious again. "You're certain you're not hurt?"

"I may be a little stiff in the morning, but nothing I can't live with. Can I call you before you go to school?"

"Why don't I call you?" she suggested. "I have to be out my front door before eight."

That was agreed upon and I said good-bye with some reluctance. It was nice to realize she was concerned about me.

The two patrol officers parked down the street. Smart, I realized. Had they parked directly in front of Harry Coats' house, they would be a target for the next out-of-control car coming off the ramp.

The older officer took my name and address, while the other one inspected my car, illuminating it with his flashlight. Harry had left the porch lights on, giving them some light but not enough for a good checkout.

As quietly as I could, I told the officer what had happened as I remembered it. When I got to the part about the werewolf, he glanced at his partner, then at me.

"Have you had anything to drink tonight, Mister Cougar?" the older one wanted to know.

"I'm in AA," I told him, suddenly irritated by the question. "Want to give me a sobriety test?"

"No need. That's just a standard question we ask everyone." Then he looked at me and grinned. "I'm in AA too. Seven years." The younger cop glanced from one of us to the other, then stepped back like we might be contaminated. The older officer, whose name tag said he was Smith, looked at him.

"What about the car?"

"There's a scar across the windshield," the young one said. "Looks like a small bore, if it was really caused by a bullet. Maybe a twenty-two magnum."

"Call the highway patrol," Smith instructed, then looked at me. "If it's a freeway shooting, they want to be involved. It's their territory."

He paused for a moment, then squinted at me. "You're the Indian that found Karen Cooley's body."

It wasn't a question. It was a matter of positive identification. I nodded as Sam Light drove up. Like the two officers, he had sense enough to park down the block and walk back. He walked past me without a glance to face Officer Smith.

"I'm Sam Light. Southland News Service." Then he glanced at me. "And you are?"

"Charlie Cougar. I'm the victim." I nodded toward the cop. "He can give you most of it. I'll fill in the blanks. What'd you say your name is?" I didn't know what kind of game we were playing, but I'd go along.

"Sam Light. Light, as in light beer." He turned back to Smith and started taking notes, as the officer gave him the basic facts from his own notebook. When done, Light turned to me.

"And you're certain the shooter looked like a were-wolf."

"It could have been Lon Chaney, Junior, I suppose, but he's still dead, isn't he?"

"This could get to be fun." Light said, trying to keep a straight face. "Werewolf," he added as he wrote it in his notebook.

"That's about all I can tell you," I said. "He pulled up beside me and drove parallel for a few seconds. When I finally looked at him, this handgun with the silencer was pointed at me. I jammed on the brakes and skidded over the divider onto the off-ramp. He kept going."

"Was the gun an automatic or a revolver?" Light was giving me the business now.

"Silencers don't work on revolvers," I told him.

"Could this have been the same werewolf that shot its accomplice in someone's backyard a night or two ago?

"I don't know," I told him. "I wasn't in the back-yard."

Light shook his head. "Might be some connection." He glanced at Smith. "Don't you think so, officer?"

Smith couldn't help smiling. "I'm just a patrol officer. I leave that up to the detectives to mull over."

"One more question, Mister Cougar. Was the werewolf male or female?"

I had to laugh then. I couldn't hold it back. I shook my head. "I'm not an expert. But Lon Chaney, Junior might know."

Straight-faced, Light closed his notebook as a California highway patrol vehicle pulled to the curb across the street and two highway patrolmen dismounted, heading toward us.

"Well, I'd better get this called in to rewrite. I doubt that it'll make the early editions." He took out a business card and wrote on the back of it. "That's my home number on the back. Call me if you think of anything more."

I didn't look at the card. Instead, I turned to face the highway patrolman who was talking to Smith and his partner. As Light sauntered away, the new arrival turned to me. In the same moment, Smith raised his hand in a signal of farewell and followed his partner to their car. After that came the same questions with my same answers. And, no, I had no idea why a werewolf would try to kill me.

When it was over, the highway patrolman called a tow truck, but he didn't stay to see its arrival. My earlier host had long since turned off his porch light and gone to bed.

A few minutes later, the truck arrived and hooked

up my car. Then there was more filling out of paper before the truck operator glanced about. "How're you gonna get home?" he wanted to know.

"I'll call a cab, if I can find a pay phone."

"Don't worry 'bout that, mister. I go right past a cabstand. Get in."

When he dropped me at the stand, it was well after eleven o'clock, and I was bushed. I gave the driver the name of the hotel, and when he frowned and shook his head, the address. Then I went to sleep.

I didn't even look in the bar as I went through the dimly lit lobby. Instead, I took the aging, hesitant elevator to my floor, and did a key fumbling act before I got into the room. Inside, I turned on the light and looked around. Everything was as I had left it.

I took off my shirt and emptied the pockets, a nightly habit so I don't lose too many tax-deductible receipts. On top of the pile was Sam Light's business card. On the back, in his familiar scrawl was written: *Call me, no matter the time.*

I pulled off my boots and settled on the edge of the bed before I started to dial his home number. Then I canceled and dialed the office on a hunch. As expected, he answered, "Southland News Service. That you, Charlie?"

"Yeah," I answered. "Thanks for the act so the fuzz didn't know I called you first."

"They probably ought to pay an entertainment tax on our routine," he agreed. "Do you have any idea what kind of gun it was?"

"I didn't have much time for study, but I think it may have been an Automag Two."

"I'm not familiar with it."

"It comes in several barrel lengths, but the longest is six inches and a sound suppressor fits real nice on it. Chambered for the .22 Winchester magnum cartridge. It's been around since the middle eighties. Assassins like it."

"How do you know all this?" Light sounded a bit disturbed that maybe I knew things he didn't.

"I worked in the Stembridge Gun Room in Hollywood for a while," I told him. "They supply a lot of the firearms and cutlery to the studios."

"Automag Two," he mused. "Probably been many thousands made."

"Not too many thousands. It's made by a small company in Irwindale, about twenty miles out. They have more success with bigger bores."

Light hesitated for a moment before he spoke. "Okay, let me think about it. Meantime, I have some news for you. As soon as I got in my car I used the phone to call the desk in San Francisco and give them the story. They'll run it in the morning edition. The papers here will have it in the afternoon."

"Sounds like good work," I offered, wondering why the urgency in his note.

"More important, I called Joe Delaney. Woke him up."

"That's no way to treat a sick man."

"He didn't mind. I asked him if Karen had ever kept any of the monster heads she created for movies. He explained that most of them were makeup jobs, not just a papier-mâché thing you pulled on over your head. But then he came up with something real interesting.

"Seems that Karen had taken one of her designs, and using real animal fur, some human hair, plastic and what-all, she created a werewolf head that could be pulled on, then zipped up the back to hold it on. She'd been trying to sell it to people who manufacture Halloween costumes."

"Then that's where the werewolf got his head," I ventured. "Has to be."

"He probably found it the night they were wrecking her house, and he put it on when he heard the cops. He didn't want to be identified."

"What about his dead buddy?"

"I don't have his name yet. They're trying to locate next of kin. Rumor is that he was some junior hood who drifted in a few months back from New Orleans, hoping to make it in big-time crime."

"Did Joe tell you where he got that silver cross he put on top of the coffin?" I asked, trying to stifle a yawn.

"I didn't think to ask. Later, I guess."

That was it. And I was asleep no more than five minutes later.

Chapter Seventeen

I was awakened from the nightmare by the shrilling of the phone beside my bed. If I wasn't awake by the time I put the receiver to my ear, I was an instant later. Sweet Sioux's usually dulcet tones were more of a snarl.

"Charlie Cougar, you lied to me!" she charged. "I won't stand for lying from anyone and that includes you!" I wanted to ask her what she was talking about, but didn't get the chance.

"You said you were run off the ramp and that's all. The radio says the werewolf tried to kill you!"

"It was only one shot," I finally managed to put in. "I wasn't hurt."

"But you were being shot at! Why didn't you tell me?"

"You were busy and I'm not supposed to call you

at work." Lame, but the only excuse I could come up with on the spur of the moment.

"You did call me at work and you lied! Lied! Lied! Lied!" She was wasting her time with computers. She would make a great prosecuting attorney.

"I did not lie," I said firmly. "I simply did not tell you all that happened."

She had calmed down a bit, but her tone was still firm and direct. "Well, you won't have the chance to forget to tell me things from now on. I don't want to see you! I don't even want to talk to you! At least, not until you quit playing Captain Adventure and grow up!"

That was it. It was 7:30, and I knew she had called just before she'd gone out the door on her way to class. I wanted to call her back, but I knew if I caught her, that would only make things worse. The big, empty hole I was feeling somewhere between my chest and my stomach couldn't get worse, though.

"Just as well," I tried to tell the image reflected in the mirror across the room. "She's spoiled and she's bossy. Maybe it's for the best." Both of us—the image and I—knew the last was not true.

When I stood up, a groan erupted from my lips. The ribs I had broken weeks ago on that shale slide gig were letting me know they did not like being mistreated as had been the case last night. A hot shower, though, and I was feeling a little better physically, if not emotionally.

Pulling on a clean pair of faded denim Levi's, visions of my nightmare came creeping back into my memory. I sat down on the edge of the bed and closed my eyes, trying to remember. I had been running through a dark jungle, the werewolf right behind me, carrying a silenced automatic. I was clutching a chain with a silver cross that I knew the monster wanted, but I didn't know why he was after it—and I didn't know why I had it.

I was running as fast as I could, but the creature was gaining. Suddenly I stumbled over a tree root and fell, still clutching the silver cross to my chest. As I rolled over, the werewolf was standing over me, and I was looking into the tube of the gun's silencer. That was when the phone had rung.

I figured Sam Light probably was on the way to his office. Rather than call him on his car phone, I decided to let him concentrate on not getting killed on the freeway.

In the lobby, I asked the desk clerk if Bob the Burglar was booked into a room. He shook his head.

"From the looks of him yesterday afternoon, he probably slept behind a billboard or under a bridge. He was out of it."

"Yeah. Or maybe in jail, where he'd be safe from himself," I added, pushing my way through the door to the coffee shop.

I don't recall what I had for breakfast. It wasn't important. Instead, I was remembering what Sue Tallfeather had said about growing up, and I couldn't help a wry chuckle. She'd probably want me to enroll in college and take computer science! The thought was supposed to carry a bit of bitterness, I think, but in my mind, it only came across as ridiculous. And it did nothing to lighten the weight that was pulling at my emotions. I suddenly wondered if I was in love, the thought fostering a tinge of fear. Fear of the unknown, maybe. I'd never had to ask myself that question before.

My damaged ribs were aching. I didn't feel like squeezing into a phone booth, so I went back up to my room to call Sam Light.

"Have you talked to Joe Delaney?" I wanted to know. "About the silver cross?"

"I just hung up. Had to run him down at his office. He was with a customer and couldn't talk. Asked if we'd come by about seven tonight."

"Both of us?" I wanted to know.

"That's what he said. You're part of this, Cougar, whether you want to be or not."

"Yeah. I know." I thought of adding that the connection had lost me my girl, but didn't. Instead, I told him about the nightmare.

"It must mean something, but what?" Light ventured.

"I don't know. If I was on the reservation, I probably could get a witch to interpret it for me."

"Either you have something the werewolf wants or you know something he doesn't want you to repeat. Since he tried to kill you, I'd say it was the latter. Or maybe he just likes to shoot people."

"Well," I told him. "I can't sit around here and think about it. I have to go run down some people."

"Want me to pick you up tonight?" Light offered.

"I don't think so. Don't know where I'll be coming from, but I'll be there about seven." I didn't bother to tell him that going out there and making a few citizens even more miserable than they probably were might help to get my mind off of Sue Tallfeather. Besides, I knew it really wouldn't make a difference.

I realized I had to get out and do something, but it was as though my mind was in a state of suspension. I wanted to talk to Sue, but I couldn't. First, I new I couldn't find her on that sprawling college campus and, second, I wasn't going to accept blame for a deed I thought of as protecting her feelings. Maybe I should have told her that the werewolf was after me. That I'd been shot at. It probably would have aroused some sympathy. Instead, she had told me to grow up.

It was nearly noon when I heaved myself off the edge of the bed and went into the bathroom to wash my face and comb my hair. I called the towing service, which also was an auto repair place. They had not had a chance to check the brake problem and asked me to call back in a couple of hours.

I found the two summonses and looked them over. One was in an apartment complex less than three blocks away, but the other was in Encino, way out in the San Fernando Valley. Each of the documents was the opening step in attempting to collect overdue credit card charges—plus the ridiculous interest. And both sets of papers apparently were made out to house-wives. I was willing to bet the husbands knew nothing about the problem. I'd been seeing too much of this over the years—easy credit leading all too often to a messy divorce.

I decided to walk up the hill to Los Feliz Drive and check out the apartment house. Maybe it would take some of the soreness out of my back muscles.

I found the place, pushed the bell on the door, and was confronted by a cute little woman in an apron. She could have been no more than twenty-one, I figured. She wore no makeup, her hair was in braids, and she was wiping flour off her hands using the bib of the apron, as she smiled at me.

"Can I help you?" she wanted to know. I noted that the screen door was still locked.

"Are you Arleine Howatte?" I asked politely. She nodded that she was and I pulled the summons from my pocket. "Is this your name right here?"

I held the document so she couldn't see her name typed on it and she unhooked the screen so she could get a closer look. As gently as possible, I put the summons in her hand, then used my own hand to close her fingers around it.

"I'm sorry, Mrs. Howatte, but you're being sued," I said quietly. I saw the initial shock, then the tears start to form in the corners of her eyes, lips quivering as she looked down at the summons. I turned away quickly. "I'm sorry to be the messenger."

As I walked back down Western Avenue, I was truly sorry for her. More and more people were getting into financial trouble, and there was no great challenge in serving them. Danny Dark had said the documents he had given me would be easy. They were that, but they also were heartbreaking.

One job like that a day was enough, I told myself. Back at the hotel, I phoned a car rental agency and told the voice that answered I needed something inexpensive for a day or two and would need to be picked up so I could come in and fill out the papers. It was agreed that I'd be standing on the curb in ten minutes.

The papers filled out and the imprint of my credit card in the rental agency's files, I drove back and parked in the hotel lot. It was almost four o'clock, still three hours before I was supposed to meet with Sam Light and Delaney. I thought of driving out to Sue's house and parking across the street where I could wait until she came home. I decided against it. If she saw me and called the cops, I'd probably be arrested as a stalker.

My stomach was offering vague rumblings, and I realized I hadn't eaten since breakfast. I walked around the corner from the parking lot, entering the coffee shop through the street door. Instead of choosing a booth, I sat at the counter, noting that all of the condiments were back in their usual positions on the back edge of the ledge. I considered ordering soup and creating my Apache stew, but I wasn't up to the effort. Instead, I ordered a medium-rare hamburger and fries. The only condiments I commandeered were the mustard and the catsup.

I drank water with the hamburger, then ordered a cup of black coffee to top it off. I was halfway through the coffee when I started abruptly and sloshed it over the counter. I had been recalling the dream once more, running from the werewolf.

"A sloppy drunk is bad enough, Cougar," the waitress muttered, as she wiped up the coffee, "but you have no excuse."

I looked up at her, smiling as I drew some folded bills from my shirt pocket. From my walking-around money, I separated enough to cover the check and a respectable tip, and shoved the bills toward her. "You'd be surprised, honey."

Back in my room, I dug into the back of my closet and found a battered briefcase saved from my rodeo days. There were some four-year-old rodeo schedules in it that I dumped in the wastebasket. Twenty minutes later, I was driving down Ventura Boulevard in the Valley, looking for a hardware store.

I spotted an Ace Hardware on a side street and pulled into the adjoining lot. It took me no more than ten minutes to find the three items I wanted. I carried them out to my rental car and put them into the briefcase, not bothering to spin the twin combination locks.

I found a phone booth and called the auto repair place. They had looked over my vehicle and found that I had somehow pulled loose a hydraulic line while going over the divider between the freeway and the off-ramp. There appeared to be no other damage. They gave me the repair price and I told them I'd be there in the morning to pick up the car.

The sun had set behind the Hollywood Hills by the time I got back to Studio City and parked in front of

Joe Delaney's house. There was a FOR SALE sign, listing a Valley realtor on the lawn in front of what had been Karen Cooley's house.

Sam Light's car was parked at the curb, and Delaney's van was in the driveway. I reached across the seat to grab my briefcase before I got out and locked the doors.

There was a few seconds' delay after I rang the bell, and I used that moment to look up and down the quiet street. Ours were the only cars parked at the curb. With the burial of Karen Cooley, the area seemed to have gone back to sleep.

It was Light who let me in, explaining that Delaney was in the bathroom. In the living room, we took the same chairs we had occupied on our first visit. A moment later, Delaney appeared. His face was white and he was walking slowly as though in pain. He offered a grimace as he lowered himself into his chair. He sat staring at us thoughtfully for a moment.

"You may've wondered why I'm willing to talk with you two and tell the rest of the press to jam it." His voice was low, almost a growl. "You two've acted like gents, not a bunch of vultures. You've treated me like a citizen, not an oddity. That's all I have to say about that."

Light nodded. "We thank you for telling us, Joe. It makes a difference." He looked at me. "Tell him the dream, Charlie."

Once again, I reiterated what had happened in the nightmare, ending with me clutching the silver cross to my chest, the werewolf about to shoot me. When I was finished, there was heavy silence as Delaney seemed to think about my tale. Finally, he shook his head.

"Doesn't mean much to me," he croaked.

"Where did you get the silver chain and cross?" I asked him.

"It came to my office the afternoon of the murder. Came by messenger."

"Why you?"

"Karen had told me on the phone she was having it delivered to me, 'cause she might not be home to sign for it. Said she was being stalked and might blow town for a time."

"When did you open the package?" Sam Light asked suddenly. He seemed to know where I was headed.

"I brought it home with me, but I didn't open it till the morning of the funeral. And I had it buried with her. Seemed fitting."

"I wish we had it," I told him. "I think the bottom cap on that cross screwed off and there probably was a message to you."

Delaney stared at me for a long moment. "You think that?"

I stood up, grabbing my briefcase. "I think it's time to adjourn to her backyard. You want to lead the way?"

Light was staring at me in speculative fashion, and I winked at him as the old mobster hoisted himself out of the chair and slowly led us out of the room, through the dining room, then the kitchen. He unlocked the back door and held the screen for us to precede him.

"I'll get the gate. It's tricky." Delaney said, and led us across the sliver of grass between his house and the high hedge. He opened a narrow gate that was almost hidden by the surrounding greenery, allowing Sam and myself to pass through.

"There's something I need in the house," he announced, closing the gate behind us. "I'll be right out."

Light and I stood there for a moment, staring at the two big plastic crosses that stood stark white in the light of a quarter moon.

"Do you know what you're doing?" Light wanted to know. I nodded and pointed at the more distant clothesline support.

"Go down there and pound on that thing," I instructed. "See if it sounds hollow."

Sudden understanding brought a nod and Light actually trotted to the opposite side of the yard. He stopped and doubled his fist, tapping on the side of the thick upright pole. It sounded hollow. That was when I turned and banged my fist against the one beside which I stood. It didn't sound the same. Their was no echo of hollowness; just the dull thump of my fist.

I opened the briefcase and handed Sam the flashlight and a set of electrician's cutting pliers. "Take down the clotheslines," I instructed. "Cut them close to the crossbars."

He stood erect, reaching up to cut the first of the lines extending between the two crosses. Carefully he laid it back so it would not interfere with what we were doing. Meanwhile, I took the new hacksaw—blade included in the price—from the briefcase. Shoving the case aside, I began to saw the plastic post just above the grass, taking care to clear the concrete into which the post was sunk.

"Think we ought to wait for Delaney?" Sam wanted to know as he cleared away another length of the plastic-covered wire.

"We're on a roll," I muttered. "Let's find out for certain."

I was about halfway through the plastic tube, but was feeling an odd resistance, when the shot came. I didn't hear it. All I heard was the bullet hitting the post only inches from my head.

I dropped the saw and started to roll away, shouting at Sam Light. As an old combat veteran, he knew what was happening and was on the ground, scuttling for the darkness of the shadows cast by the high hedge. The gun was silenced, I realized, but I could hear the slam of the bolt as it drove forward for the next shot. That was all.

Then came a loud report from the hedge line, and I saw the yellow-blue muzzle flash of a heavy caliber firearm. Right behind it came two more shots from the same weapon. In the back area of the yard, I heard a grunt, then a thrashing sound.

The silenced shot into the pole had caused the pole to swing about, the action breaking my saw blade. Lying there, I watched as the pole swung away, still held by two of the clotheslines on the far side. When it fell to the ground, bits of paper bounced out of the hollow bottom.

I don't know how long we lay there, waiting for more shots, but there were none. Finally, I heard the gate squeak and looked up to see Joe Delaney come through.

"I got him," he growled, starting toward the rear of the yard, hands carrying what looked to be an old Ruger .44 Magnum carbine. He held the firearm at the ready as the two of us fell in behind him. As we reached the rear border of the yard, where still another hedge rose above our heads, Light aimed the flashlight to shine into the growth. A body was hunched face-down amid the tangle, part of the silenced handgun protruding from beneath it.

"Pull him out of there," Delaney ordered. Between us, Sam and I managed to drag the body into the Cooley yard and turn it over. Sam unzipped the werewolf mask and pulled it off.

"I figgered it was him," Delaney muttered. "I shoulda killed him a long time ago."

Danny Dark stared up at us with cold, hard eyes that were just beginning to glaze over in death. His lips were twisted in a sneer.

Chapter Eighteen

In the ten days or so since the slayer of Karen Cooley had been taken out, there had been a flurry of legal outrage from the district attorney and staff when Joe Delaney was released on $200,000 bail. His crime, it seemed, was not that he had shot Danny Dark and settled the unsolved murder of Karen Cooley. According to the DA, Joe was a convicted two-time felon. Under the law, he was not supposed to own a gun, have access to one, or even so much as touch one. And under California law, three convictions for violent felonies means life in prison without parole.

The people who were involved on the Federal level, of course, were agents of the Bureau of Alcohol, Tobacco and Firearms. It was a law they really didn't know how to handle, considering the circumstances.

Had it not been for Joe Delaney firing through his hedge, both Sam Light and I probably would be dead.

While we waited for the cops the night he had shot Danny Dark, he explained several things that had a bearing on what had happened. After Dark had shot his own accomplice in Karen's backyard, Joe had gone out the next morning and inspected the hedge through which he had escaped. He had found an area that had been used for a stakeout by Dark. He had figured Dark would be there that night, knowing I was getting close to figuring out where the money was.

Joe Delaney was sure Dark had killed Mac Calley and disposed of the body. As studio production manager, Dark had been Calley's inside man at Metropolitan Pictures, furnishing him with info and aiding in the scam. According to Joe, Calley was supposed to split the money with Dark, but seemed to have ignored the fact while he was gathering up his assets in cash.

Delaney had been bailed out by a bondsman and had told a group of reporters that he had no intention of spending his final months in a jail cell, dying by inches, while the legal beagles tried to figure out what to do with him. That said, he had gone back to his house, where he had another gun hidden in a wall. He had kicked out the wall, recovered the gun, and killed himself as they say. His death had ended his problems.

As it turned out, the summons Danny Dark had given me to serve Karen Cooley was as phoney as a three-dollar bill. He had made up the papers himself, faked signatures, and had used me to run down the woman he thought could lead him either to Mac Calley or to his money. Throughout the entire project, he had been using me, gaining bits of information from my reports and my verbal comments in his office. I was not sorry that he'd bought the farm, as they say, there in the late Miss Cooley's backyard.

Of course, a new wrinkle bothering the local lawyers and politicians had to do with what they termed "proper disposition" of the $2,000,000 that had been stuffed into the plastic cross.

An attorney named Max Weiss lived two doors from Karen Cooley and had returned from an extended vacation in the Orient to learn what was going on. It was he who had drafted a will for the retired stripper before he had gone abroad. In fact, it had been his teenage son who dug the holes, set up the clothesline supports, and concreted them in. Karen had paid him $200, which had gone into the young man's college fund. Questioned by Sam Light, then the police, the young man said one of the PVC upright supports had been considerably heavier than the other. Karen must have packed it full of Mac's money herself.

As for Karen Cooley's will, the lawyer contended, there were some serious problems. If Mac Calley turned up, he could argue with the law about his money. However, if he didn't turn up within the seven-year limit, he could be declared legally dead. Since his disappearance predated his sister's murder, Max Weiss argued, as his next of kin, the money should become part of her estate to be held in escrow until the seven years was up.

As Weiss told the press at the conference he called, "This is going to present a legal entanglement that may take years of court proceedings and landmark decisions. There is no doubt that some of Mac Calley's money came from legal investments. As for racketeering charges, he was not tried and convicted before his death, so he must be considered innocent of such charges."

I really began to think well of the late Karen Cooley when I had a chance to read a copy of the will. She had a cool, I-don't-really-care attitude that was refreshing amid all the greed that had surrounded her. Under the terms of her will, her personal funds and the money from the real holdings would be split among established homes for unwed mothers located in three different states.

The kicker was a clause in which she stated that should her estate come into money after her death, it was to be used to establish a home for retired, ill or down-on-their-luck exotic dancers. The home was to be established in Danville, Illinois, once considered the strip capital of the world. In its heyday, the community not only had a dozen or more clubs and burlesque palaces catering to a clientele of tourists, students from the nearby University of Illinois, and local farm workers, but it also was headquarters for the booking agents who handled the exotic talent for operators all over the nation.

The sad note was that Karen Cooley apparently had given up her hope that her brother might still be alive somewhere.

On a more practical note, with Danny Dark among the recently departed, I figured I was going to have to find another way of paying for my day-to-day living costs while I was waiting for someone to start making cowboy and Indian pictures again. In fact, I'd settle for a film with just an Indian cast!

Over the years a few producers had tried stories that dealt only with Indians and they had been box office disappointments. These projects did better on television.

With the whole thing pretty well wrapped up and Sam Light getting credit for some very exclusive reporting, he had been called to San Francisco to talk with his bosses. He was hoping they'd give him at least one more reporter to help with the bureau. He also had put through a voucher in the amount of $2,500 for my services. I had the check in the bank and felt temporarily secure.

With Sam gone, there was no one I could bounce my personal problems off of. I thought of Bob the Burglar, but he was in no shape to listen to anyone about anything, according to reports off the street. He'd gone through his paycheck and was borrowing money wherever he could.

I suddenly realized I was a loner who didn't want to be alone. I wanted to talk to Sweet Sioux too, about some of the things she had said. She thought I should get into something permanent instead of booming around, trying to serve people and risking getting shot at the same time. Things could be a lot better between us. I had more than a vague feeling that I was on probation with her and I didn't like the sensation. I'm an Indian and supposed to be a free spirit. She's an Indian too, and should feel the same way, but doesn't. Some romance!

Chapter Nineteen

I hadn't done much during the preceding week beyond trying to maintain a low image and stay away from the press people. I had thought maybe my involvement in the Danny Dark thing might make my name ring a bell with some of the town's casting directors, but no such luck. I was surprised when I found a note in my mail slot to call Myrtle at the Dark office. What could she want?

When her number answered, it wasn't Myrtle on the other end. It was a voice with a good deal more charm. I told her who I was and she said, "Oh, yes. Myrtle has been trying to reach you. I'll transfer you right away."

I mulled that until the rough tones I remembered reverberated in my ear. "Where've you been, Cougar?" she demanded. "I've got work for you!"

I shook my head, staring at the wall of the hotel room for a moment. "What's this all about?" I demanded.

"I'm running Dark's business now," she growled at me. "I gave him free rent and telephone service, so I was always a silent partner. Seems he left me the business in his will."

"Crazy!" I muttered.

"Yeah. Ain't it!" There was a sharp laugh. "But I need you and a couple of those other clowns who worked for him. And I especially need you now!"

My checking account usually wondered how soon bankruptcy would rear its ugly head, but with the money from Sam's newspaper, I was in fair shape. Still, I had to do something besides sit in a hotel room. I told her I was on the way.

Dark's name was gone from the frosted glass door and replaced by gold letters that spelled MYRTLE K. GREEN. She was seated behind Dark's desk, going through a stack of file folders. She looked at me and shook her head.

"He sure didn't know much about running a business," she said. "No wonder he turned into a crook!" Then she slid one folder off the top of a thin stack.

"I've got a real goodie for you, Charlie."

"Oh no," I moaned. "You sound just like Dark when he was about to pass me something impossible. It better not be another Karen Cooley."

She shook her head, extending the folder toward me. "Nothing like that."

"If you saved it and sent for me, it has to be a real

gem." I ventured a quick look at the summons. Apparently, this individual had an ex-wife who wanted to discuss a lot of back alimony in front of a judge. "Where am I supposed to start looking for him?"

"He's a grave digger." She smiled a smile I had never seen before. I didn't know her all that well, but for a moment I thought she was joking. Then I knew she wasn't. "He works at the Shady Rest Pet Cemetery."

"Where's that?" I wanted to know. The question got me a shrug.

"I don't know. You get paid to find out." She was still smiling as she waved me toward the door. "On your way, Cougar!"

I asked the new switchboard operator if she could locate a number for the Shady Rest Pet Cemetery. While I paced up and down the office, she tried all of the Los Angeles area phone directories and drew a blank.

"Sorry I can't help you," she apologized. Her phone was ringing and she took the call while I waited. Apparently, it was someone to whom Danny Dark had owed money. I figured it was going to be a long call, so I waved as I departed.

I had charged out after the call to Myrtle with neither a shower nor breakfast. I needed both, so I walked the few blocks back to the Heartbreak Hotel. The mid-morning sun on my back told me the afternoon was going to be a scorcher.

I went through the shower and put on a clean pair of Levi's, an aging T-shirt that advertised an Indian rodeo from a half dozen years back, and pulled on my cowboy boots. I started out the door, then went back to my closet and found the Western-styled Bailey straw hat I had worn off and on for a lot of years.

I stopped at the desk and asked the clerk if he knew anything about pet cemeteries. That got me a shake of the head and the comment, "Cougar, you've got a strange sense of humor."

In the coffee shop, I found Bob the Burglar at the counter, staring into a nearly empty cup. I tried to avoid him, but he saw me and motioned to the stool beside his own.

"Where you been?" he wanted to know.

"Don't you read the newspapers?"

He shook his head. "Not this week. I was busy with a drunk."

"Anyone I know?"

"Me. Just me."

I took a longer look at him. He appeared to be sober, but there were deep rings of darkness discoloring the skin below his eyes. He also had a split lip that looked painful.

"You fall down or someone slug you?" I asked. He shook his head.

"I don't know." There was a pause and I took advantage of it to look at a menu that I probably had memorized. I ordered eggs, bacon, and hash browns, with coffee.

"Suppose you could stake me to breakfast, Charlie?" Bob's tone was reluctant and I knew he hated to ask. Even alcoholics have some pride.

"Go ahead and order," I instructed, glancing at the waitress who still waited. "You know where to find the Shady Rest Pet Cemetery?"

"I stay as far away from graveyards as I can," she replied as she wrote down whatever it was Bob had ordered.

As she walked away, I glanced at Bob again. He was staring at me with an expression I couldn't translate.

"I think I'm ready now," he said quietly.

"Ready for what?" I wanted him to say it.

"For one of them AA meetings. Will you take me?"

I nodded. "Lost your job at Columbia?"

"Lost everything but my head," he muttered. "I've had it."

"Can you stay sober till six o'clock tonight?" I wanted to know. He thought about it, then nodded.

"See me here at six and I'll take you, but I'm not going to wet nurse you. It's pretty much up to you." I figured out later that I was being selfish, covering my own conscience in case he didn't make it. I guess we all do that sort of thing sometimes.

We ate in silence and I gripped his shoulder as I picked up his check along with my own and went to the cash register. The same waitress took my money, glancing at me as she handed me my change. "Why a pet cemetery?" she wanted to know.

"That's where you find the people." She had her mouth open as I walked out.

In the hotel's phone booth, I sorted out the change I had in my pocket. I found I was not the only one who did not know where the Shady Rest Pet Cemetery was located. I first called a couple of pet stores. They thought I was joking. Then I tried two people-type morticians. They thought I was a weirdo. Two veterinarians tried to give me the address of the Los Angeles Pet Cemetery that they thought was run by the county. That didn't help. Neither did someone at the county coroner's office when I called there.

I tried to call Sam Light, but his assistant said he was at the courthouse. She didn't know when he'd be back. I could hear her computer clacking as she talked to me.

Then it struck me. I didn't know what Sue Tallfeather's schedule might be, but I called her at home, hoping she'd be there. She was.

"Well!" she said. "Finally, I hear from you!"

"Life has been totally complicated the last few days."

"I know," she said. "I do read the newspapers."

"And after our last discussion, I wasn't certain you wanted to hear from me."

"Look, Cougar, what we had was a discussion, not a lovers' quarrel," she announced. "I'll let you know when that's going to happen."

"You mean we're going to be lovers?" I knew I shouldn't have asked.

"I'll let you know whether that's going to happen too," she announced, trying not to laugh. Suddenly I felt better. "Why are you calling?

"I need help."

"I thought you were the self-sufficient brave, the slayer of enemies, the hunter of buffalo!"

"Sue," I said carefully, "I need you to get into your computer and see if you can locate an outfit called the Shady Rest Pet Cemetery."

There was a long pause. "Is this another Captain Adventure gig?" she finally asked.

"Just trying to help a friend." It wasn't exactly a lie.

"Call me back in twenty minutes," she instructed finally and hung up. I went back into the coffee shop to see if Bob the Burglar wanted to ride with me, but he was gone. I hoped he'd be there at six, as he'd said.

I drank another cup of coffee, checking my watch every few minutes. When I called back, Sue answered immediately. "It's a private pet cemetery down in Orange County. Not too far from Disneyland." She gave me a chance to dig a pen and my notebook out of my shirt pocket, then gave me the address, followed by instructions on how to get there.

"You've convinced me, Sue. I need you."

"I truly hope so. I think we need each other," she said softly and hung up.

I pondered that statement all the way to the upper reaches of Orange County. Commitment was something I had long avoided. In the past, if some lady had even suggested I commit myself, I had run. With Sue Tallfeather, I didn't feel at all like running.

I found Beach Boulevard just as Sue had said I would and soon spotted my goal. I pulled into an area covering several acres and braked long enough to look it over. There were thousands of small tombstones and monuments sprouting from the carefully clipped ground. The stones were set close enough together, indicating it didn't take much room to bury a dog or cat.

Probably fifty yards away, not far from the gravel drive, four members of a family—well, mourners, at least—were gathered around a small coffin. It was no more than two-feet long and appeared to be fashioned from mahogany. I didn't learn until later that some pet coffins sell for as much as $500!

Looking past the man, woman, and two youngsters, all with heads bowed, I saw that there were fresh flowers on some of the other graves, and I saw Oriental prayer wheels on others. Beside one of them an old lady sat on the grass, gazing morosely at the tombstone. I suddenly was engulfed by a slow, creeping sensation I didn't like.

And off in the distance, almost at the rear fence, I could see a guy in overalls who was digging a hole with a long-handled shovel. Unless this one was a grave robber, he had to be my man.

I drove to within about thirty yards, then stopped my car and got out. I paused to look about, seeming to study the parklike surroundings. I wanted to appear to be a man who needed a grave dug. I had his summons tucked in my hip pocket. It would be out of sight as long as I was facing him.

I was maybe a dozen feet from the man when he looked up and paused to glare at me. A tall, skinny man who resembled the late John Carradine, he fit the role of a grave digger perfectly. Inspired type casting!

I asked his name and he suddenly brought the round-nosed spade up to hold it at port arms as a soldier might his rifle. I began to wish I had brought a gun.

I asked his name once more and he still didn't answer. Instead, he used both hands to throw the shovel in my direction. As I dodged this missile, he turned and ran with a long, galloping stride. I sprinted after him, dodging around tombstones, leaping over them, trying to cut him off.

Cowboy boots aren't designed for running and I felt my toe connect with one of the small rectangles of granite before I went tail over tea kettle, digging up about a yard of the carefully planted sod with my face.

When I finally looked up, trying to blink the grass and dirt out of my eyes, I couldn't help muttering, "Sue, you're right. I need a different line of work."

I was staring at the inscription on one of the miniature tombstones. The weathered but still legible inscription read:

WE LOVE YOU, CHARLIE
REST IN ETERNAL PEACE

Slowly, I rolled over on my back and stared at the cloudless blue sky. Someone besides Sue Tallfeather was trying to tell me something!